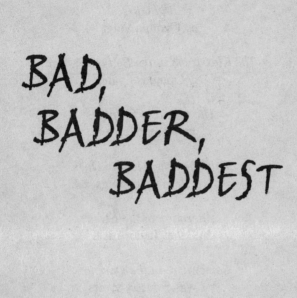

APPLE SIGNATURE

BAD, BADDER, BADDEST

CYNTHIA VOIGT

SCHOLASTIC INC.
New York Toronto London Auckland Sydney
Mexico City New Delhi Hong Kong

For Lucia del Sol Knight,
an excellent bad girl,
and her best friend Bob

ISBN 0-439-08096-7

12 11 10 9 8 7 6 5 4 3 2   9/9 0 1 2 3 4/0

Printed in the U.S.A.   40

First Scholastic Trade paperback printing, August 1999

I.

Bad News

"They can't *do* this to me!"

Mikey's whisper split like the skin on an over-ripe tomato.

"Girls," the librarian warned them. The librarian's desk in the Reference Room was right in the middle, so she could keep an eye on everything.

"They can't!" Mikey whispered angrily.

"Quiet," the librarian said. "Please."

Margalo was crawling along beside the bottom shelf that held the volumes of American biographies. She didn't say anything. Mikey was always angry about some *this* some *they*s were doing.

Margalo had enough troubles of her own; she didn't need any additions from Mikey. She had only this hour after school to take notes about Eleanor Roosevelt from the Reference Room books and to find enough books in the stacks to add enough titles to her bibliography to convince Miss Brinson that she had spent three homework weeks on the report. Margalo sighed. Of course she hadn't spent three weeks; she didn't need to. If she'd needed to, then she would have. But teachers didn't think like that. Teachers acted as if everybody should take the same amount of time getting the same job done. Students who took longer were slow. Students who took less time were hasty, and probably careless.

Margalo sighed again. Miss Brinson was new at teaching, and young, and seemed easygoing, but more than once in the first weeks of school she had proved unexpectedly smart. So Margalo wasn't about to let Mikey distract her from getting her work done.

Once she'd finished the report, Margalo could pay attention to whatever was bothering Mikey, and start looking forward to Doucelle's slumber birthday party on Saturday, and before that to a Friday night sleepover at Mikey's. Mrs. Elsinger had promised to make lasagna. But first there was this report to be written.

Mikey poked Margalo in the ribs.

Margalo ignored her.

Mikey punched Margalo — pretty gently, actually — on the shoulder.

Margalo just moved away, out of fist range.

The Elsingers had their own private encyclopedia, so Mikey could look up Bonnie Parker at home. Besides, Mikey was making up most of her report from a video she had seen last summer, at her grandmother's house. Bonnie Parker was a crook, with her boyfriend, back in the thirties, and somebody had made a movie about them. She was a female gangster, which was why Mikey liked her. Did that make her a gangsta? Gangstette? Gangstress? If Margalo hadn't been ignoring Mikey, she'd have cracked the joke at her.

"Margalo!" Mikey complained, as Margalo pulled the QUE–RUS volume out from the shelf.

"Shhh." Both girls looked up at the librarian, who put a finger against her lips.

Mikey smiled at her.

The librarian knew Mikey and didn't smile back. She pointed to the SILENCE, PLEASE sign hanging off the front of her desk.

Margalo took the encyclopedia volume to the

table, where Mikey's backpack had been dropped beside hers. Mikey followed.

"You have to help me stop them!" Mikey whispered urgently.

"I have to read this article," Margalo whispered back.

"Xerox it."

The librarian cleared her throat, her eyes fixed on them.

"I don't have any money," Margalo whispered.

"I do," Mikey said, and grabbed up the volume.

The librarian warned them. "Margalo?"

Mikey looked over and nodded her head at the librarian. She mimed opening the big volume, then mimed turning it upside down, mimed putting a dime in a slot, pressing a button. She mimed watching a copier at work copying an encyclopedia page.

The librarian looked confused.

Mikey headed for the glass doors. Margalo tried to retrieve her book. "I've got *work* to do," she whispered.

"Margalo," the librarian warned them again, so Margalo — who was used by now to the way teachers and librarians and parents and any passing adult always called on her when Mikey made trouble — went up to the desk, to explain. "I need to copy something," she whispered.

"The reference books can't leave the Reference Room."

Mikey had already left the room, carrying the QUE–RUS volume.

"I'm doing a report on Eleanor Roosevelt," Margalo whispered.

"It's a rule," the librarian whispered back.

"For Miss Brinson's sixth grade, at George Washington Elementary," Margalo whispered.

"It's a library rule," whispered the librarian.

"My report's due Friday."

"These books are extremely expensive. I don't think you know how expensive they are."

"I'm sorry," Margalo whispered.

"Well." The librarian gave up. "It's not as if the high price of books is your fault." She looked through the glass doors over to the two copiers, at one of which Mikey stood.

Margalo carried their backpacks out of the Reference Room. "Finished?" Mikey greeted her. "I am." She handed Margalo the Xeroxed pages.

"Aren't you going to put the encyclopedia back?"

"Why should I? It's your report."

Margalo was taller than Mikey, who was shorter and thicker, so Margalo looked down into Mikey's round face, and brown eyes, until Mikey couldn't pretend she didn't get it.

"I don't remember where it was on the shelves," Mikey argued. "I'm not the one who knows exactly where to put it back."

Margalo decided to try negotiation. "You do that and I'll pick out a couple more biographies, of her or F.D.R., and check them out so we can wait for Aurora outside."

Usually Mikey avoided deals and went for exactly what she wanted, but this day was an exception. So Margalo knew that there really was something serious going on.

Outside and able to talk in normal voices, the two girls sat on the curb where Margalo's mother couldn't miss them. Cars drew up to let people off, or went on to park in the big lot behind the library. People walked by, coming and going. The sun sank lower in the sky. Margalo knew Mikey was waiting to be asked, and that's why she didn't ask. She thought she could probably hold out longer than Mikey, so she sat there, her heels pulled close to the curb and her knees up high, and her arms around her knees, waiting.

She didn't look at Mikey, who was picking chips out of the crumbling cement of the curb.

Finally Mikey demanded, "Aren't you even curious?"

Margalo smirked a little victory smirk.

"What if I have to move away?" Mikey threatened.

Margalo's smirk faded.

Mikey grinned then, a big *gotcha* smile.

"Is your mother changing jobs again?" Margalo asked.

Mikey started from the beginning. "They can't do this to me!" she proclaimed.

"Who?" Margalo asked. "Who can't? Do what?"

Usually when Mikey said "They can't do this to me," she was talking about something like France testing nuclear weapons in the South Pacific, or the school board increasing the number of school days in a year. "They can't do this to me" was what she usually said whenever anybody talked about making abortions illegal again. "You aren't thinking of getting pregnant, are you?" Margalo would usually ask her, and Mikey would usually say, "Don't be stupid."

Margalo didn't think she was being stupid. She thought she was being subtle, reminding Mikey that the whole world didn't revolve around Michelle Elsinger. But this cool October afternoon wasn't one of the usual times; Margalo was beginning to get that. "What's going on?" she asked. "Tell me."

It was getting chilly, getting dark. Margalo hoped Aurora hadn't forgotten that she was picking them up. "Who they?" she asked again. "What who?"

"Them," Mikey said. She was busy watching the toes of her sneakers. "Him. Her."

These were Mikey's parents.

"What have they done now?"

"They haven't done anything. Yet. But, you've been divorced, I want to ask you — "

"They're getting divorced?" When people got divorced, families broke up. When families broke up, somebody moved out of town.

"I can't tell if they are or aren't. They talked to me." Mikey couldn't sit still. "Last night." She jumped up and walked around the library lawn. Margalo trailed at her shoulder.

Both girls wore jeans, long-sleeved polos, sweaters, and sneakers. Mikey's sweater was a patchwork of bright colors, bought in a boutique that sold expensive clothing made by hand in South and Central American villages. Margalo's speckled black-and-white pullover came from the New-to-You Shop, price one fifty. On the other hand, Mikey's sweater made her look like a bright plastic beach ball — which Margalo didn't tell her. After all, sometimes the best thing for a friend to do was keep her mouth shut. And besides, Margalo liked to see Mikey bouncing around in that beach-ball sweater, looking jolly and friendly.

Because jolly and friendly were two things Mikey wasn't.

"They say they're only *thinking* about getting a divorce," Mikey muttered over her shoulder. Then she stopped in her tracks, wheeled around. "A trial separation, maybe." She glared at Margalo, her mouth fixed in a toothy smile.

Mikey was growing her hair long again, and wore it in a little short ponytail that looked bouncy and cute. Two more things Mikey wasn't.

"Why do they want to get divorced?"

"They said, they don't love each other anymore," Mikey answered impatiently. "*I* could have told them that. But so what?"

"Well," Margalo said. "It probably matters to them."

"What about me?" Mikey demanded. "What about what matters to me? I'm their obligation, aren't I? At least until I'm eighteen and can legally live on my own."

"That's seven years," Margalo said.

"Six and a half," Mikey — who was better at math — corrected her. Margalo was only better at spelling.

"Does this mean I can't sleep over on Friday?" Margalo asked.

"Absolutely not," Mikey said. "You've got to."

"I don't know," Margalo hesitated. She'd been in the same house with a divorce before, and it wasn't any fun. Mikey was leading them around behind the library, walking fast.

"She's making lasagna," Mikey reminded Margalo.

Mrs. Elsinger might be a disappointing mother for Mikey, and a disappoint*ed* mother, too, but she was a great cook.

Margalo tucked her shoulder-length hair behind her ears and thought about divorce.

"I'll ask her to make tiramisu," Mikey added. "She feels guilty, so she might. This is a secret," Mikey told Margalo.

"What is?" Margalo asked, and then she answered herself. "The divorce? Of course. But maybe they won't do it. But if they do," she burst out with her real question, "will you move away?"

"Not if I can help it," Mikey said, smiling the kind of smile that made Margalo step back out of fist range. "That's why you've got to come over on Friday, just like normal, and pretend you don't know anything. You have to figure out how to stop them."

They had circled the library and now they sat down again at the curb, legs stuck out into the roadway. Light faded from the sky.

Mikey groused, "People shouldn't just have children then break up the kid's home. It's irresponsible. It's like *your* mother. And how do you know she won't do it again, with Steven?"

"Because," Margalo said. Steven was Margalo's second stepfather, but the best father she'd had.

"Yeah. Right. Because," Mikey mimicked. "Good logic." She looked Margalo right in the face. "Because why?"

Margalo shrugged.

"What makes you think your family's immune?"

"I didn't say that."

"She's done it twice before."

"I know."

"Aurora. What kind of name is that for a mother? No wonder she keeps getting divorced."

"Talk about bad logic," Margalo said. "You're just jealous," she said.

"So what?" Mikey asked. "I am not," she argued. "Not much."

"They both like having kids around," Margalo said.

"They must, with all seven of you."

"Actually, nine," Margalo said. "Counting everyone."

"I could come live with you," Mikey offered. "Howie and Esther have done it."

"Howie and Esther were already her stepchildren, that's why, and they asked to stay with her."

"She could charge my parents child support. That would give you more money."

Margalo didn't say anything.

Mikey knew an impossible idea when she heard it. Even if she was the one saying it. "Besides, I'm *their* responsibility. They can't go farming me off on someone else."

"Maybe they aren't really going to," Margalo said.

"How can you tell when parents are really going to?" Mikey asked. "You've been divorced, even not counting your father because you were so young when he went off."

Margalo shrugged. "It just — gets to be the only thing they *can* do." She tried to remember exactly what happened with Harold Lightower, Esther and Howie's father, at the end. She hadn't been paying much attention to him; she'd always just counted on Aurora. "He was never home, he didn't ever want to come home."

"And who would I live with?" Mikey said. "Usually it's the mother, and if a mother doesn't get custody, people wonder what's wrong with her, so Mom would ask for custody, so people would know she was a good mother. But she doesn't like living with me."

"Your father likes you. Doesn't he?" Margalo asked.

"I think so. I mean, he gave up getting stoned for me, he says — and he hasn't, not once, since we moved here. And that's over a year ago," Mikey said. "But he knows Mom would kill him, and besides, he promised. I don't really blame her, do you? For not staying in love with him. He is sort of a dork. Mr. Cornflake, soggy with milk."

"But if you have to live with her . . ."

"She couldn't turn me into her ideal Barbie doll dream daughter, do you think? Not in only six and a half years. What could she do, anyway? Just more of the same, more nagging about diet camps and baby-sitting and the nice little girls whose parents she met at work for me to be friends with, so I'll have more friends. My mother's not sure about you," Mikey said.

"I know," Margalo said. "I'll take that as a compliment."

They were grinning at one another when Aurora pulled up. When she saw the rusty Nova approaching, Mikey's face turned serious. "Don't tell, not anyone. Not even your mother, not even Steven." Then she stood and picked up her backpack. "You promised," she reminded Margalo.

Margalo didn't think she had promised. She'd given her word, but she hadn't promised. She'd keep her word, but she hadn't made any promises she had to keep. "No I didn't," she said.

The two little kids were the only other people in the car, strapped into their side-by-side car seats. Mikey got into the back, with them. There was a rule: The person whose mother it was had to sit in the front with her. The rear of the station wagon was filled with plastic grocery bags, all of them stuffed full. Mikey had given up trying to get Aurora to use canvas shopping bags. "Hey, Stevie," she said. "Hey, Lily."

"What about me?" Aurora asked, and "Hey, Aurora," Margalo said, strapping herself in. "Boy, did I drop a bundle at the supermarket," Aurora said. "Maybe we should become vegetarians. How do you feel about being a vegetarian, hon?"

"Maybe we should become bank robbers," Margalo answered.

"You don't make that much robbing banks," Mikey told them, from the backseat. "Bonnie and Clyde never got more than fifteen hundred dollars from a heist."

"Back then, wasn't fifteen hundred dollars worth a lot?" Aurora asked, signaling. She always drove slowly, cautiously, because she always had children in the car with her. Sometimes Mikey wanted to climb into the front and push Aurora's foot down harder on the accelerator.

"It wasn't that much, even back then," Mikey said, as if she knew what she was talking about. Aurora would believe her, and maybe she was right, anyway. "Bonnie was really ripped off. She had a lot more criminal ability than that."

Aurora waited to let two cars out ahead of her, and asked, "You two have a slumber party Saturday, don't you? Are you coming to our house Friday?" She looked at Mikey in the mirror.

"I'm going to hers," Margalo told her mother.

Mikey said, "I think Clyde held her back. I think if she'd been running around with Pretty Boy Floyd, for instance, she'd have done better."

"Choosing the right man is important," Aurora agreed, pulling slowly out into traffic. "Or, at least, not staying with a wrong one."

"They didn't have any children," Mikey pointed out.

The phone rang while Margalo was dumping her books out onto her bed. She ran to the hall to grab up the receiver. "You don't think it's my fault, do you?" Mikey asked. "Because it isn't. You know that. Except, if I'd had some brothers and sisters, they might like being *their* parents. I should have had brothers and sisters."

"Wait a minute." Margalo took the phone into the bathroom, which luckily nobody was in, so that she couldn't be overheard. "When are they going to decide?"

"You tell me. I thought she was so busy trying to fix me, she wouldn't notice him. I guess I haven't been bad enough for her. Maybe I could get some horrible disease. That would bring them together."

Mikey wasn't making any sense, so it wouldn't do Margalo any good to try to talk sense to her. "I've got to work on my report," Margalo said, which was true.

"What about me?"

"You have to do your own report."

"Not funny, Margalo."

"Yes it is."

There was a silence from Mikey's end of the phone.

Margalo gave in. "I can't think of anything, not now, but I'm not trying."

"When will you try?"

"After I've finished my Eleanor Roosevelt

report, Mikey. I have priorities," Margalo said.

"Tomorrow?" Mikey asked.

"Good-bye," Margalo said. "Someone wants the bathroom."

It was Howie Lightower, her stepbrother from her mother's second marriage, the only experience of an older sibling Margalo had had until her mother married Steven MacLeish, who was about twelve years older than Aurora, so his youngest child, Susannah, was four years older than Margalo, and also older than Howie. But when Aurora was married to Harold, before she married Steven, Howie was the oldest. "Who's in there?" Howie called, knocking at the door. Margalo reached over to flush the toilet, then ran water in the sink as if she was washing her hands. Eventually she opened the bathroom door and carried the phone out to its table.

"About time," Howie said.

The phone rang again. Margalo could guess who it was.

"When you had your divorces, how long did it take?" Mikey asked.

"The last time? I was five, I don't remember. But I thought you said they were just thinking about just separating."

"Why are you whispering?"

"I'm in the hall. Howie's in the bathroom."

"Spare me the details," Mikey said. "All of you in one bathroom. I don't like to think about it."

"Not the babies," Margalo pointed out. "Not Steven and Aurora."

"That's true," Mikey went sarcastic. "How could I forget? That makes it only — what? Only seventeen of you using one bathroom?" Mikey didn't agree with Aurora and Steven about how many children a couple should have, in this over-populated world.

"You know it's only five," Margalo said. Besides, Aurora and Steven weren't going to have any more; they'd fixed that, and Mikey knew it. So she didn't see why Mikey didn't just stop her nagging on the subject. It wasn't as if you could return a baby to the store it came from and get your money back.

"Five is too many, *that's* what I know. *They* aren't sure, but I am. Pretty sure."

"What, exactly, did they say when they talked to you?"

"She said — he didn't say a word and I don't know what *that* means — 'Mikey dear.' A dead giveaway, 'Mikey dear.' That's what she'll say when she wants to tell me my dog is dead."

"You don't have a dog," Margalo reminded

Mikey. " 'Mikey dear' — then what?"

" 'Your father and I' — another trouble phrase — 'your father and I have been talking about it, and we think it might be for the best if we were to try living apart.' Her exact words."

Margalo tried to see some reason for hope. "She didn't say they're definitely going to."

"But she likes to break bad news slowly. You should have heard her when they decided to move here. Hint, hint, lie. Hint, lie — it took her *weeks*. She doesn't want me getting overexcited. You know how she feels about overexcitement. You'd think, in that case, she'd be completely happy with him."

"So she's the one who wants a divorce?"

"He runs away from things, anything rather than face them, so I can't imagine him cooking up this caper. Can you?"

Margalo couldn't.

"I don't know why she married him in the first place. He's not her type."

"What do you know about that?"

"I know why Steven's Aurora's type. They both drool all over kids and abandoned kittens. But my dad doesn't care if he ever gets a promotion, or a raise. He hasn't got anything to drool over. Not golf. Not the house. Not his job, which he hates, and he holds that against her."

"Because she made him leave his old job?"

"And why shouldn't she have? It was a great opportunity for her, and his business was still struggling. But I don't think he's happy. Can grown-ups be unhappy like a kid can? Always unhappy? Like Lindsey, depressed?"

"Lindsey's not depressed. She's depress*ing*."

"And I'd be depressed, too, if I was her. You're right, Margalo. Things could be worse. I could be Lindsey Westerburg. I think if they get a divorce, he'll be on my side."

"So you think they're going to."

"Don't tell."

"I said I wouldn't."

"Not even Esther."

"Why would I tell Esther?"

At the sound of her name, ten-year-old Esther Lightower put her head around the bedroom door. "Are you talking about me?"

Margalo shook her head, listening to Mikey say, "Esther thinks I'm a hero. She follows me around. You know that."

"Who are you talking to?" Esther demanded.

"Mikey," Margalo said.

"What?" Mikey asked.

"No, I'm talking to Esther."

"What's she saying about me?" Esther asked.

"I told you not to," Mikey said.

"Not about *that*," Margalo protested into the phone.

"Not about what?" Esther demanded.

"Just go away," Margalo said.

"I will assume you meant that for Esther. Say hi for me," Mikey said.

"Mikey says hi."

Esther reached for the receiver. "Let me talk to her."

Margalo turned her back to Esther and the hall, leaning up against the wall as if she was shielding the phone from gunfire.

"I'm telling," Esther said. "Mo-o-om!" She followed her voice down the stairs. "Margalo won't . . ."

"Remember, it's a secret," Mikey said.

"You don't need to tell me a hundred times."

"Promise. You have to promise."

Margalo gave in. "I promise." Margalo whispered, because if she was overheard making a promise, they would know she had a secret, and they would try to worm it out of her, all of her stepbrothers and stepsisters.

"Why are you whispering?"

"I'm not alone."

"You're never alone in your house," Mikey said.

She hung up without saying good-bye. Mikey never said good-bye on the phone. She just hung up. Sometimes she hung up when Margalo was in the middle of saying something.

Sometimes, but not always, Margalo would call back to finish what she was saying.

"Off the phone, Margalo," her mother called up from the kitchen.

Margalo replaced the receiver in its cradle. "I already am," she called down.

"It's been more than five minutes," Aurora called up. The five-minute limit on phone calls was Steven's way to give everyone equal phone access.

"I'm already off," Margalo yelled down, over the sound of radio from the girls' room, where Susannah was probably doing homework, and stereo from the boys' room. Ziggy Marley? she guessed.

The boys' door opened and Howie stuck his head out. The volume of music increased, dancy, bubbling. "What does a person have to do to keep things quiet around here?" Howie asked her.

Margalo didn't let Howie intimidate her and she didn't let him trick her into quarreling, as if she wanted to win some fight about who was making more noise. She just looked him in the eye.

That always worked with Howie, giving him the fish eye.

"How long until dinner, anyway?" he finally asked.

"No idea," Margalo said, and went down the first two steps. She stopped, turned around, and called up to Howie's back as he returned to his room, "Five minutes?"

That wasn't true, but he'd stop whatever he was working on, turn off his music, turn off his mind, and be downstairs ready to eat before he found out the truth. He'd be furious.

"How long until dinner?" she asked her mother as she entered the kitchen.

Sesame Street was on the TV. Lily was sitting on a little plastic chair, watching. Stevie, who was four, stood up close at one side of the set, running one of his cars over the screen. Aurora had the TV in the kitchen, where she usually was, but she refused to watch the evening news, and she didn't want her children watching it either. Aurora was antiviolence.

"Can you set the table? Esther, go out back and tell Steven — they're painting that cat shelter they've been working on — tell them it's time to start putting things away. Tell them, it's almost supper, everybody should wash their hands. Is your report going all right, hon? And don't forget soup spoons. We're having stew and the little kids need spoons for the gravy. Biscuits, too, so when you're finished with the table, take down a platter, because by that time the biscuits should — I *think* the box said twenty-five minutes, do you want to see if you can find it in the garbage and check? Then tell me if you think I need another can of carrots in the stew, because I put in an extra can of gravy, because the little kids eat it like soup."

Twenty minutes later they were all eating, and talking away about where everyone could go stay when Steven and Aurora went to an out-of-town wedding at the end of the month, convincing Esther that the cats would do just fine left alone for a weekend, that being one of the things an outdoor cat shelter was useful for, and trying to listen to Stevie's long story about Mr. Rogers and the truck, when the phone rang. Susannah jumped up to answer it. Steven looked across the table at Aurora, raised his eyebrows in mock surprise, and asked, "Do I take it there's a new boyfriend?"

"There's always a new boyfriend," David answered. He was seventeen and a senior, and he'd about had it — as he often said — trying to keep his boy-crazy younger sister from making seven kinds of fool of herself over her crush of the moment. Not to mention embarrassing him, being a constant embarrassment the way she stood around trying to flirt as if she was some kind of sex goddess. Couldn't Aurora *talk* to her? He didn't take Aurora's word for it that Susannah wouldn't be that way for long, or his father's word for it that most boys tried to treat a girl decently, especially if they were friends of her brother. David had lost faith in everyone in his family, the way they let Susannah behave.

Lily turned her bowl of stew upside down and leaned over the edge of her high chair to see it puddle onto the floor. "Oh," she said. "Look. Lily made water."

"Doesn't look like water to me," Howie said. "Looks like throw up, doesn't it, Dave?" He elbowed David.

"Fall," Lily finished her sentence. Lily was not to be distracted from finishing her own sentences.

"Phone's for you, like always," Susannah said to Margalo, nearly stepping into the spilled stew. "Who did *that*?"

"I fall," Lily announced proudly.

Aurora was mopping the floor with a paper towel while Steven served Lily more stew and Esther announced that if they had a dog the dog would clean it up, and Stevie — who hadn't yet figured out that a dog was about the last thing the family needed — said he wanted a beagle.

"It's Mikey, big surprise," Susannah said, sitting down.

Margalo ran up the stairs.

"Are you having dinner?"

"Yes."

"What're you having?"

"Stew."

"Dinty Moore?"

Mikey was sometimes pretty sarcastic about Aurora's cooking habits.

"No, homemade. Except for the canned potatoes and frozen peas and canned carrots in it. She cooked the meat herself. And canned gravy."

"I just thought, the way your family starts talking. You know how you talk," Mikey said. "All of you, and you, too. So don't."

Then she hung up. She had delivered her message.

Margalo stood looking at the receiver for a few seconds, before she slammed it down.

2.

A Messy Evening

At the end of detention on Friday, Mikey and Margalo came through the school doors running. You didn't keep Mrs. Elsinger waiting.

Mrs. Elsinger had something to say to her daughter. "Someday," she said, "that school — "

She jammed on the brakes at the stop sign at the end of the school drive, glanced over her shoulder, and punched the accelerator.

The car leaped out onto the road.

"That school is going to — "

A red light halted the Audi just inches from the rear of a Cherokee.

"Lose patience. With you, and just expel you."

Hemmed in ahead and behind, the car couldn't move, temporarily. Margalo loosened her grip on the seat belt.

"And then where'll you be?" Mrs. Elsinger asked Mikey.

Who didn't inform her mother that this time, as sometimes happened, it was Margalo who had been given detention. Margalo had shaved two or three minutes a day off of her time in math class by coming just a little late from recess. Miss Brinson worked it out: In just the first four weeks of school, Margalo had already missed almost an entire math class. Margalo hadn't argued with her teacher; she'd already done the multiplication. She was just sorry Miss Brinson caught on so quickly. Margalo and Mikey both used the detention time to get their weekend homework done; except Mikey had to sit out in the hall, with her books on the floor around her, while Margalo got her own library table, because she'd been bad.

The light turned green and Mrs. Elsinger started honking — *blat* — *blat* — *blat*. "What's wrong with these zombies?" she demanded.

"To start with, if they're zombies they're dead," Mikey told her mother.

"You know what I mean."

The car spurted forward. Two cars, four, whipped backward past Margalo's window as if they were being sucked up by some alien vacuum cleaner from outer space. Then Mrs. Elsinger darted into the passing lane and charged up to the next red light.

Margalo loosened her grip again.

Mrs. Elsinger's fingers tapped on the steering wheel. "Why'd you bring a sleeping bag, Margalo? Is Mikey's room even worse than usual?" she asked.

And zipped under the stoplight just as it switched to green, gaining two car lengths on a Civic.

Mikey rolled her eyes and sighed sarcastically. "It's Doucelle's party tomorrow. You remember, she's having a slumber party for her birthday. You remember, you were so excited I was finally invited to a slumber party, you got me the Dead tape to give her, the final concert. What are you giving her, Margalo?"

"A mix tape," Margalo said. "I put in a couple of David's favorite cuts. Howie picked one for me.

Almost everybody gave me something, Aurora, Steven, Susannah. Esther wanted 'Puff.' Of course."

" 'Puff the Magic Dragon'?" Mrs. Elsinger asked. "I loved that song."

"You didn't do it," Mikey told Margalo.

"No, I told Esther she could give it to you, on your birthday."

Mikey smiled, lots of teeth.

"Aren't you girls too young for tapes?" Mrs. Elsinger asked.

"You tell me," Mikey answered. "You're the age expert."

"Young for sarcasm, too. We didn't get sarcastic until ninth grade, at least. It's Friday." Mrs. Elsinger slipped the car into a NO PARKING, BUS STOP space across the street from the bank. "Payday. Long lines. First the bank, then the grocery store. Greens," she explained, although nobody had asked. "Fruit for dessert."

"I thought we were having tiramisu," Mikey said. "I *asked*."

"Just because you ask for something doesn't mean you'll get it," her mother answered. "One of us has to watch your weight."

Mrs. Elsinger mothered the same way she drove — darting, swooping, parking wherever she wanted to. She knew where she wanted to get to, and she planned to get there quickly, to get it over with.

After her mother had gone, leaving the motor running, Mikey turned around in her seat to ask, "How does she seem to you?"

"Normal," Margalo said. "Normal for an investment banker, that is. Normal for her."

Mikey stared at Margalo, who stared right back at her. Most people, when Mikey stared at them, found other things to look at. Not Margalo.

Then Margalo's eyes got mischievous, and smiley, before the smile moved down to her mouth. "If a policeman comes along — you'll have to drive away. You'll have to, if we see one coming."

"It would be a meter maid."

"You ought to sit in the driver's seat. Just in case."

Mikey could imagine what her mother would have to say about somebody else sitting in her driver's seat. "I can't drive," she pointed out.

"What's so hard about driving?" Margalo asked, practically daring her. "This is an automatic. It's not like you'd even have to know how to shift."

Mikey looked out the rear window, hoping to see a meter maid.

But the driver's door opened and Mrs. Elsinger tossed her big purse across onto Mikey's lap.

Fastening her seat belt with one hand, she pulled out into traffic.

Many horns honked.

Mrs. Elsinger honked right back. "I don't know what *they're* complaining about."

"I do," Mikey said.

"And I wish you'd let me make an appointment to get your hair cut. Instead of going around looking like some drug dealer. With that hairdo. I'll tell you, *I'd* give you detention, just for the way you look."

"I don't look like a drug dealer. I look like I live in L.A. Drug dealers have short hair, and they wear suits. Drug dealers look like bankers."

"You watch too much TV," Mrs. Elsinger decided. "I don't know where you're watching all that TV," she said, looking at Margalo in the rearview mirror.

Margalo wished she'd look at the road.

At the supermarket parking lot Mrs. Elsinger swooped down on a parking space in the front row, heading right for the green Geo that was heading for the same spot.

The Geo braked, and backed off.

"I wish you wouldn't quarrel with everything I say," her mother told Mikey. "And I can't think of why — with all the other possibilities — you had to do your report on Bonnie Parker. Who did Margalo do?"

"Eleanor Roosevelt," Margalo told her.

"See what I mean?" While she talked, Mrs. Elsinger unbelted herself and took her purse off Mikey's lap. "But I really don't know why that Miss Brinson gave you the permission."

"She didn't," Mikey said.

Margalo grinned.

Mrs. Elsinger stopped moving, and turned to face her daughter. "Oh, Mikey. Now you'll flunk the assignment."

"I hope not," Mikey said.

"And it'll serve you right. If that Miss Brinson has any smarts, she'll make you do the whole thing over, start to finish. I don't know why you can't do things right the first time and spare me the misery." She straightened her shoulders, made very broad by the pads in her suit jacket, and got on with her life. "These things catch up with you," she warned Mikey. "Talk some sense into her, Margalo, will you? You're a good influence."

"Thank you," Margalo said, trying not to laugh, and Mikey said at the same time, "She is *not*."

Mrs. Elsinger had already flung the car door shut and moved off.

"Why don't you just tell her Miss Brinson said

we could write about anyone we wanted?"

"Why didn't she *ask* me? And why did they have a kid if they're not going to stay married?" Mikey answered. "I won't let them get away with it."

"You can't really stop them."

"It's a secret," Mikey reminded her. "It's *my* secret."

"I have a brain, you know. Not a colander," Margalo said.

"A colander separates out the good stuff. You should *want* a brain like a colander," Mikey argued.

"Never *mind*," Margalo said. Sometimes she sympathized with Mrs. Elsinger, trying to get Mikey to listen. "Just never mind."

"No, I'm right. But let's argue about that some other time." Mikey was cheering up. She knew she was driving Margalo crazy. "What I want you to do today is watch them. Observe."

"Do I have to?" Margalo asked.

"That's a joke, isn't it?" Mikey asked. "It is," she decided. "You have to watch them and figure them out, like Nancy Drew. Nancy Drew them at dinner, then tell me what their secrets are. You're good at that kind of stuff."

Actually, that sounded sort of like fun, except

Margalo wasn't at all sure she wanted to know the Elsingers' secrets. Grown-ups' secrets weren't the same as kids'. They tended to be messy, and more serious, whereas kids' were mostly just embarrassing.

But if she could figure out what was going wrong with the marriage, then Mikey wouldn't move away. Mikey moving away would leave a big hole in Margalo's life; and especially now that she was getting close to junior high, and high school, which were real trouble areas. Mine fields, that's what junior and senior high schools were, from what she'd seen at home. Margalo figured, she would rather cross a mine field not alone. If you crossed it alone, then if anyone got blown up it would be you. If you crossed it with somebody else, your chances of being the one blown up got halved.

Margalo was curious to hear what Mikey thought about junior and senior high, but Mikey was fixated on the divorce question.

And Margalo could see why.

After they carried the canvas bags of groceries into the house, Mikey went back outside to kick the soccer ball around. "You don't like soccer," she told Margalo, which was true enough.

Mrs. Elsinger was putting away groceries and heating up the lasagna she'd made the night before; she had no time to care what Mikey and Margalo did.

"You want a snack," Mikey told Margalo, and left her there in the kitchen. Margalo knew that what Mikey meant was *I want you to find out as much as you can from my mother*, but she went to Mikey's room instead. Mikey's room was behind the kitchen, at the opposite end of the house from her parents' room. "Quarantine," Mikey called her room, because her parents kept out of it, as if Mikey's messy habits might be catching.

Margalo shoved piles of clothing onto the floor and lay down on Mikey's bed to listen to Phish for a while. Then she went back into the kitchen, where Mrs. Elsinger had *All Things Considered* on the radio while she cooked. Margalo went outside.

Mikey footed the ball through the open garage door, followed the ball in, and came out dribbling it. She'd worked up a sweat. "Have you decided what you think?"

"Not yet. I haven't even seen him. But if I were your father, I'm not sure I'd want to be married to her."

"He doesn't. And she doesn't want to be married to him. But that's *their* problem, not mine. My problem is keeping them from getting divorced. She does that — gets her mind set on something and — *bam* — that's it. That's how we moved here. She had a friend who got mugged, and — *bam* — the city wasn't safe — as if it had been safe before — but — *bam* — she finds a better job — *bam*, *bam* — Dad has to quit his company, I have to change schools. It was practically overnight, and she expected everything to be perfect as soon as we moved. I bet now she thinks getting divorced will make things perfect. Could she actually believe that?"

"How would I know?" Margalo asked, but then she relented. "Some people keep trying for perfect even if they say they know it's impossible. Like, for example, people who practice soccer all the time."

"Why shouldn't I?" Mikey demanded. "You're jealous," she said.

Margalo denied it. "Am not. Not of that."

Mikey caught the ball she was about to drop-kick and looked at Margalo. "Then what?"

Margalo went for the obvious. "Your stereo." She looked at Mikey's round face. "Your thick hair."

Mikey drop-kicked the ball into the garage. They heard it thunk against the side of the Audi. "I'm not jealous of *your* hair," she said. "There

comes Dad. Go check them out when they're together. You said you would."

"*You* said I *had* to," Margalo corrected her.

"I didn't say you *had* to," Mikey argued.

"It's what you meant," Margalo said.

"So, are you going in?" Mikey insisted.

Margalo went inside.

Mrs. Elsinger had almost finished cleaning up
the cooking area. She had a wooden bowl filled
with greens ready to be dressed, a glass measuring
cup of vinaigrette, the lasagna — Margalo could
smell it — in the oven, a loaf of bread wrapped in
aluminum foil ready to be warmed, and the table
set for four people.

"What's she doing?" Mrs. Elsinger asked.

"Practicing goal shots. I think," Margalo reported.

"I don't know." Mrs. Elsinger looked out the
window. "I don't know about you girls," she said,
and then she added, still looking out the window,
"There he comes, Mr. Cornflake, right on the dot.
He's turning into Mr. Corn*puff*, don't you think,
Margalo?"

Margalo drifted toward the door to Mikey's
room, in case she wanted to make a quick exit.

Mr. Elsinger entered through the back door, a
big, broad man, wearing a gray suit and carrying

a black attaché case. "T.G.I.F.," he said. "I need a drink. Hey, Margalo, what's new? What's for dinner, Supermom? Is that lasagna I smell?"

He didn't even slow down for an answer. He walked on through the room, and when he came back, he had taken off his jacket and tie and left the attaché case behind somewhere. Mr. Elsinger didn't move like a man who wore suits and ties to work, and tie shoes; he moved like someone who had miles to go, and only his feet to take him there, and was wearing good boots. He did look like a Mr. Cornflake — healthy, strong, maybe not as smart as he might be. That wasn't what he *was* like, but it was what he looked like. Margalo didn't think he'd put on so much weight.

"How about a snort, Margalo?" Mr. Elsinger asked. "Name your poison. Supermom? What can I do you?"

"You know I don't like being called that," Mrs. Elsinger said.

"A martini," Margalo said.

"In your dreams," Mr. Elsinger told her. "How about some nice prune juice?"

"I've asked you not to, more than once," Mrs. Elsinger said. "More than twice. I'll have San Pellegrino, with lime. And ice."

Margalo couldn't taste the difference between

one kind of water and another, but she loved to go home and talk about bottled drinking water, and bread with foreign names — baguette, focaccia — so "Me too," she said.

"You two are a real party," Mr. Elsinger said. He gave Margalo one tall glass of bubbling water with ice cubes and a chunk of green lime, and carried the other one over to his wife, who stood with her back against the sink. Mrs. Elsinger looked him in the face when she took her glass —

Woo-oo-woo-ee.

Margalo could almost see the anger, like an invisible force field. If it were a visible force field the anger would be black, huge, a Doberman pinscher attacking.

Mr. Elsinger drew back, like a cornflake would with a bite taken out of it if cornflakes could try to get away from chomping teeth. Surprised, too, was Margalo's guess. But why would he be surprised? Unless there were things Mrs. Elsinger hadn't told him, but if they were talking about divorce, what kinds of things would a wife still not tell her husband? Margalo wondered.

This detecting stuff was interesting.

Mrs. Elsinger smiled at her husband then, and said, "Bad day at work, sorry," but she said it with a glance at Margalo, so he'd know that she'd apologized only because Margalo was there. Then she went to the back door to call Mikey in. It was time for the news.

The Elsingers watched the evening news together, from six to six thirty, and then ate dinner together; they were a family. Mrs. Elsinger wouldn't have a TV in her kitchen, so they watched the news in the den, where a long couch faced a big TV with a built-in VCR. Margalo sat quiet while various terrible events flashed on the screen, then flashed off. News stories never lasted long, unless there'd been only one disaster that day, or it was something like the O.J. Simpson trial. Mikey muttered comments — "That liar," or "Must be a slow night if this is the worst they can come up with." They all sat in a row on the sofa, like condemned prisoners facing a firing squad, Margalo, then Mikey, then Mrs. Elsinger, then Mr. Elsinger. The TV set faced back at them, ready to shoot.

Margalo glanced sideways at Mikey's parents, checking them out. They kept their eyes fixed on the TV screen. When it switched from showing starving people — or dead people, or powerful, important people — to showing ads, the Elsingers didn't move or change expression. They watched everything with the same alert attention. Bright, cheery ads sold things to eat or to drive, while dramatic ads sold medicines, as if a headache was as bad as a brain tumor. Maybe that was the Elsingers' trouble — they didn't know the difference between a headache and a brain tumor, a Big Mac and Bosnia?

During dinner Margalo relaxed on the detecting to concentrate on the lasagna. The Elsingers and their maybe divorce would wait, but she liked her lasagna hot. The mild and sweet rich taste of cheeses, topped with the sharp and meaty taste of tomato sauce, underlined with the pale and solid taste of thick pasta . . . Margalo cut off bites, slowly, and carried them to her mouth, slowly, on her fork; and she chewed them, slowly, as slowly and savoringly as she could.

She'd gotten a big helping, about twice as much as Mikey and more, even, than Mr. Elsinger. When Mr. Elsinger asked for seconds, his wife frowned across the table at him. "I thought we'd agreed you were going to try to eat less."

"You agreed," he said. "You told me I should and didn't wait for me to have my own opinion. C'mon, Patty, lighten up. What's the point of being a great cook if you won't let me eat?"

He passed her his plate. She dropped a small serving of lasagna onto it. Then Mikey passed her plate for seconds and Mrs. Elsinger frowned again.

Margalo frowned too, trying to see if there would be enough for seconds for her.

"But you refuse to come with me to the health club," Mrs. Elsinger said.

"I work hard all day. I want to relax when I get home."

"Are you implying that I *don't* work hard?"

"I wouldn't dare," he said.

The Second Ice Age was starting at Mrs. Elsinger's end of the table and moving glaciers down toward her husband.

Mikey's fork clattered onto the floor beside her. She bent down to pick it up. "It's okay, there wasn't any food on it," she reassured her mother. "I'll blow the germs off." She blew through the fork at her mother, smiling.

"I was thinking of going over to the health club tonight, if you don't have any plans," Mrs. Elsinger said.

"You're already going tomorrow, and Sunday afternoon," Mr. Elsinger pointed out.

"Do you have a problem with that?"

"If I were the jealous type I might. If I were the jealous type, I might wonder if you had a boyfriend."

Mikey slid down in her chair and kicked Margalo in the shins.

Margalo didn't need any kicking. She was

staring at her plate, ripping a chunk of bread in half as if she were splitting an atom and didn't want to blow up the world by mistake, listening as hard as she could.

"How would I make time for a boyfriend, if I even wanted one?" Mrs. Elsinger asked. "And I wouldn't want a *boy*friend, anyway, if I was looking. I'd be looking at men. If I was looking. Which I'm not."

Margalo was almost twelve and had been through one national and a couple of local elections where she was old enough to catch what went on. She knew what grown-up liars sounded like when they wanted to keep their secrets secret and still get what they wanted. Aha, Detective Margalo exclaimed, silently.

The salad bowl clattered and tipped sideways. Mikey had pulled it over to serve herself, and now a mound of dressed greens spilled out on the table.

"Oh. Sorry," Mikey said, reaching to clean up the mess.

"Not with your napkin," Mrs. Elsinger said. "The oil will never wash out, if you use your napkin."

Margalo was already on her way to get paper towels.

As they mopped up, Mr. Elsinger served himself

salad from what was left and asked, "Do you two
girls want to go to the movies tomorrow night?
Want to go to the movies with an old man?"

"You know, Anders, I'd like it if you'd come
with me and work out," Mrs. Elsinger said.

"I know you would, but would I?" he asked,
and turned back to Mikey.

"You're not old," Mikey objected, and "What's
playing?" Margalo asked, and Mrs. Elsinger said,
"Nothing over a PG rating," and Mr. Elsinger said,
"Yes, massa," and she got up from the table, if they
would Excuse Her Please.

Mikey tossed a greasy, scrunched paper towel
onto Margalo's plate.

Margalo tossed it back, onto Mikey's lap.

"Don't play with your food," Mrs. Elsinger said
as she left the room.

"So, no movies," Mr. Elsinger said.

"We're going to a slumber party tomorrow
night anyway," Margalo told him.

"Really? You too, Mikey?"

"It's Doucelle Scott's birthday," Mikey said.

"I remember, but you didn't tell me it's a slumber party. Are you excited? You'll have a good
time," Mr. Elsinger assured Mikey. "Girls love
slumber parties."

Mrs. Elsinger returned to the kitchen, her sport

bag over her shoulder. "You look healthier already," her husband said to her.

She ignored him. "And what do you girls have planned for tonight?"

"A movie," Mikey said. The Elsinger bookcase was as good as a video rental store, except free, which made it even better; so it was easy for Mrs. Elsinger to believe what she was being told.

"If you make popcorn, don't leave the kitchen a mess."

"Margalo will take care of it," Mikey promised.

"What movie?" Mrs. Elsinger asked, delaying her exit, as if now that she was about to go, she wanted them to think she didn't want to leave. *"Beauty and the Beast?"*

It was sort of sad, Margalo thought, the way Mrs. Elsinger acted as if, if she controlled the television set, Mikey would have a perfect childhood. It was pretty stupid, for someone who was so smart, but kind of sweet.

"Mrs. Doubtfire," Mikey said.

"You always watch that," Mr. Elsinger objected.

Mikey responded, "Some pleasures never fade."

"Name me one," her father answered. "Name me just one." But he was looking at his wife when he said that.

Mikey hesitated, caught out lipping off; then

she smiled her *gotcha* smile. "*Mrs. Doubtfire.*" Her father laughed.

"Okay, that's one," he said, to his wife.

Mrs. Elsinger stood at the back door, staring at her husband because she didn't like what he'd said. Mr. Elsinger went back to eating. He pushed salad greens around his plate with his fork, as if he was a South American torturer and the lettuce knew where the rebel troops had their camps.

Detective Margalo watched them both.

Mrs. Elsinger smiled at her husband from the doorway.

It wasn't a nice smile.

Mrs. Elsinger kept on smiling, waiting for her husband to look up and see how much she didn't like what he'd said.

Mikey's glass of water spilled.

What happened was, when Mikey reached for the basket of sliced bread, her arm hit her water glass, and the glass — still half full — fell over, with a clattering of half-melted ice cubes.

"Oh, Mikey," her mother said. "Not again. It's just one mess after another with you."

"Oops," Mikey said.

"I'll get a sponge," Margalo offered.

"I'll get a dish towel," Mikey offered.

"Use paper towels," Mrs. Elsinger said.

Margalo wondered why she didn't just leave.

"You can watch the movie with the girls, Anders," Mrs. Elsinger suggested.

The water puddled at the center of the table.

"Maybe I will," Mr. Elsinger said.

Margalo mopped at the spilled water. She hoped she was wearing a normal face.

"It'll be more interesting than spending the evening with a lot of people who have bricks between their ears," Mr. Elsinger said.

Mikey mopped too.

"Mr. Cornpuff and the girls watching *Mrs. Doubtfire*," Mrs. Elsinger said, and opened the back door. "Now there's a picture."

"If that's — " Mr. Elsinger said.

Reaching over to clean up the last scattered drops, Mikey hit Margalo's water glass. It tottered, and before she could catch it, it splashed water onto Margalo's salad, and her sweater, too.

"I can't take any more of this," Mrs. Elsinger said, at the same time that Mr. Elsinger said, "This is beginning to get through to me."

They both left the room.

Mikey smiled her teeth at Margalo.

Margalo didn't need to be any detective genius to figure out that things were pretty bad with the Elsingers' marriage. She rolled her eyes at Mikey.

She didn't need to be any Nancy-Drew, Detective-Margalo-on-the-job. For her money, the case was solved.

Of course, she didn't have any money.

They'd finished the dishes, and Margalo was wiping the counters clean while Mikey had the less demanding task of wiping off the table, when Mr. Elsinger came in. He'd changed into jeans and an Irish sweater. He said, Did they mind if he went to see a friend for a couple of hours?

He smiled at them, Mr. Cornflake, the kind of smile that asked you to say yes and not ask questions.

"I don't mind," Mikey said, not looking up.

"You don't mind being left alone?"

"I'm not alone. Margalo's here."

"You're sure you don't mind?"

Margalo stepped in. "We can call all our friends and party."

"All what friends?" Mikey asked, and Mr. Elsinger said, "You're a pair of fresh kids."

"So don't worry about us, Dad. Of course, you might worry about your house. . . ."

"Too big for your britches," he said happily. "Both of you. Catch you later, okay?"

"Sure," they said. They both knew he wouldn't, that he wouldn't get home until early in the morning. They didn't know where he would have gone — maybe a bar, to drink beer and watch sports on a giant TV, out with the guys, or maybe to pick up a girl? They didn't know. But they did know he wouldn't come home until late — or early, depending on your point of view.

"So, what do you think?" Mikey asked when he'd left.

"Things look pretty bad," Margalo said.

Mikey rubbed at the table with a sponge; then she turned around to glare at Margalo. "Don't tell *anyone*."

"I won't. I haven't."

"All right," Mikey said. She was in charge again. "We better put in the movie so we can say we watched it." There was no sense in wasting good lies. They'd see the first five minutes of *Mrs. Doubtfire*, but they were actually going to watch *Tales from the Crypt*, which was on Mrs. Elsinger's TV hit list. "You might as well subscribe to the *National Enquirer*," she said, but when Mikey asked, "Can I?" Mrs. Elsinger just said, "You know what I mean." Of course Mikey knew what she meant, but that wasn't the point.

"You do the popcorn," Margalo told Mikey. "I'll

melt butter," because Mikey tended to forget the butter and burn it.

Mikey poured kernels into the container part of their hot-air no-fat popcorn maker. She put the lid on top and pushed the start button. As they heated up, the yellow kernels stirred sleepily, then hopped little hops up, getting excited. Mikey watched them. It was like the population explosion, babies being born, and then exploding into grown-up size until the whole world was as crowded as the popcorn container. It's about time to start finding other habitable planets, she thought, with all the little popcorn faces pressed against the plastic, practically staring at her.

Margalo got out the popcorn bowl. Mikey dumped the popcorn into it. Margalo poured butter on top and stirred it around with her hands. Mikey salted it and stirred it around with her hands. They went to the den and sat on the sofa with the bowl of popcorn between them and no paper towel, or paper napkin, no anything but their jeans to wipe their hands on.

That was the reason you wore jeans, wasn't it? Because it didn't matter what kind of crud you got on them.

At nine they returned to the kitchen, to make sure they left it clean enough.

Margalo looked at the popcorn maker. "I won-der," she said. Then she waited.

Mikey waited too. Margalo let the *I wonder* dangle like a worm on a hook, until Mikey gave up and asked, "Wonder what?"

"I wonder," Margalo said again, running hot water into the buttery popcorn bowl. "Don't you wonder what would happen if we left the top off?"

"No."

Mikey knew what would happen. There would be a mess and her mother would get angry. Or, actually, her mother would get angrier. She was already angry — about Mikey's hair, Mikey's weight, Mikey's attitude, Mikey's father.

Then Mikey pictured what might happen when the kernels exploded into popcorn if the top was off — like spaceships going where no popcorn had ever gone before — like rats jumping off a sinking ship — and she had always wanted to see if it happened in real life the way it did in movies, if you put way too much detergent into a washing machine. This was almost the same as overloading a washer. Mikey smiled.

"You look like a wolf," Margalo remarked.

"I am a wolf." Mikey fitted the container back onto the base.

"What big teeth you have, Granny."

"The better to eat you with." Mikey kept on smiling as she poured in kernels.

Margalo pointed out, "But you have to be a man to be a wolf."

"Who says? I figure," Mikey made it up as she went along, "I want to know how to be a wolf by the time I get to high school. High school is going to be bad," she told Margalo. "I'd rather be one of the wolves there than one of the sheep."

"A wolf in sheep's clothing," Margalo suggested.

"A wolf," Mikey insisted. "In wolf's clothing. With wolf teeth."

"Are you going to turn it on? Or what?" Margalo demanded. Margalo thought maybe it would look like fireworks, exploding fireworks of popcorn; that was her hope; or like a Coke shooting out when you shook up the can before you pulled the tab.

"You can be a wolf in snake's clothing," Mikey offered. She flipped on the switch.

They watched, and waited. The machine whirred and hummed, like a miniature vacuum cleaner.

"We'll both be wolves," Mikey called, over the noise.

Margalo nodded happily. If they were both

wolves, it didn't matter what their clothing was. "They'd better look out for us."

As long as Mikey's parents didn't get divorced and move Mikey away. The trouble with divorces was the messes they left behind.

In their plastic cage, the kernels got restless, first, then hoppy; then they stirred around on the hot surface, like jumpers on a trampoline trying to work up momentum. A little hop, then a bounce almost halfway up the side — Margalo thought she'd pick a favorite and cheer it on. "Come on, little kernel!" But it was hard to tell one kernel from another. It was impossible to keep your eye on your favorite.

More of them were trying to leap up, like fleas on a flea-infested rug. Hop. Jump. Al-most.

Margalo and Mikey watched.

At last one yellow kernel exploded white, and flew up, free — shot up and into the air. It bounced on the countertop. Another followed it, ricocheting against a closed cupboard door, then over to the stove top, where it rebounded around before falling down onto the floor. And three, four, six more were escaping at the same time.

This was terrific.

This was a terrific idea.

After the first few escapes, nothing much

happened for a while. Then, with a pop, a white popped piece lifted itself up barely above the lip of the container, but fell back inside.

Too bad.

A few more kernels popped, and then — all at once — there was a mass flight of popped corn. The white fluffy kernels came stampeding up out of the top of the machine, an erupting popcorn volcano, popcorn lava. They pattered down onto the counter, onto the floor, onto the stove top. They rolled along the counter and the floor as if they were cockroaches looking for places to hide, white, fluffy cockroaches, albino cockroaches, albino overweight cockroaches. It was a mess.

"Think they could hit the ceiling?" Mikey asked. "I bet you a quarter one can hit the ceiling."

"I don't have any money," Margalo reminded Mikey, and then she started to laugh.

Popped corn bounced up out of the topless container. Now here, now there, never where you'd guess, not a whole wave of them, just more than anyone could smother down. Pop, hop, jump, bounce — all of them busting out, busting loose.

There were popped corns all over the place. Mikey and Margalo were doubled over, laughing.

The popping sounds slowed down in the container until all Mikey and Margalo could hear was the machine's contented humming. "Great," Mikey said. "That was great."

Margalo picked up a few pieces from the counter and ate them. "Yeah."

"Now we better clean — but what do you think would happen if I put fewer kernels in? I really put a lot in this time. What if I did fewer, or started it with the top on, to let things build up? Then took the top off. Would they really explode, do you think? Really explode out? We should try that before we clean up. You don't want to have to clean up twice."

"If you had a dog, the dog would have already cleaned up most of the floor."

"If I had a dog, I'd be in a different family," Mikey pointed out. "Do your cats clean up spills?"

"Cats don't clean anything, except themselves," Margalo said. "Are you going to try it?"

Of course Mikey was, and did, and of course cleaning up took longer than they planned, and so of course Mrs. Elsinger came in and interrupted them.

"Now what have you done?" she asked, and then told them, "You forgot to put the top on," and asked Mikey, "What is wrong with you?"

Margalo swept while Mikey sponged.

"There are some there, under the table," Mrs.

Elsinger said. She bent down to scrabble at some popped kernels hiding out under the refrigerator.

"I don't need this," she said. "How can I possibly give you permission to baby-sit when you get up to a trick like this?"

"I'm not asking you to," Mikey said.

Mrs. Elsinger groused on. "I don't know where your father's gone. My kitchen is a wreck. Why don't you two just go on to bed. I'll take care of this. It'll be quicker if I do it myself."

"Actually," Margalo said, "it'll be quicker if we do it together," but at the look on Mrs. Elsinger's face, she and Mikey set down their broom and sponge and left the room.

They didn't break out laughing again until they were safe in Mikey's bedroom, with the door closed behind them. They closed the door and broke out laughing, because Mikey's room looked a lot like the kitchen, only with clothes, and books, and tapes, and stuff all over it, not popcorn. Neither Margalo nor Mikey minded that. In fact, Mikey maintained that neat made her nervous; she would much rather have things messy.

Detective Margalo thought that was lucky, because her guess was that pretty soon, things were going to get pretty messy all over the Elsingers' house.

3.

Am I Having a Good Time Yet?

Late the next afternoon, Mrs. Elsinger drove them to Doucelle's house. "Don't ruin this for yourself," she advised her daughter.

Mikey turned around to cross her eyes at Margalo.

"They're girls, they'll want to talk about boys. Gossiping and giggling, that's what slumber parties are about. I remember, we practiced using makeup, tried new hairstyles, talked about boys, clothes. And our parents," she added, in a different voice.

The car halted abruptly in front of an older, shingled house, a square house with a big yard that stretched out in front and around the sides. All the houses on the street had big yards.

"And we danced," Mrs. Elsinger said, cheerfully nostalgic again. "We practiced new dance steps — for when we went to dances."

"I want to go home," Mikey said.

"No you don't," Mrs. Elsinger told her.

Margalo piped up from the backseat, "Maybe we'll do ballroom."

Mikey turned around and smiled, a big-bad-wolf smile, lots of teeth, nothing nice to it.

Before Mikey and Margalo, carrying sleeping bags, pillows, and presents, were halfway up the sidewalk, the Audi was on its way. Mrs. Elsinger had a racquetball game to get to.

Margalo reached for the doorbell, but Mikey stopped her. "Do you know why Doucelle invited us? It's not as if she likes me."

"I was sort of surprised when she called," Margalo admitted. "But she said you'd be there. I wonder," Margalo said.

"Wonder what?"

"Why she asked you first."

"Maybe," Mikey pointed out, "she wanted me more."

"Alphabetical order?" Margalo suggested. "I wonder."

Mikey waited a couple of seconds, then "Wonder what?" she asked impatiently.

"Who else will be there."

"If you don't ring the bell, we'll never find out."

They both knew there would be eight guests, since Doucelle had explained to them her father's formula for the number of people who could attend a birthday, including the birthday girl. Or boy, if it was her older brother, Richie. The number had to do with her new age — which, starting with age eleven, had to be added together to make a single digit — added to the grade she was in. This meant that her fourth-grade party had the most people she was ever allowed to invite — Mikey had worked that out — but eighth grade would be second best, with thirteen. "That'll be some sleepover," Mikey had said to Doucelle, who had answered, "Unless I want to have a boy-girl party, instead."

Mikey had stared at her.

"But probably I won't," Doucelle had said.

Among the eight guests, there were two surprises. Surprise One was who wasn't there: Linny. Linny was the class queen, which nobody said and everybody knew. For a class queen, Linny was okay, not too stuck up with her own popularity.

She wasn't too smart, or adventurous, too funny or
fresh, or too polite, either — she wasn't very anything. Margalo thought that was why everyone
liked her. "I don't," Mikey said. "Do you?" When
Margalo said, "Sure, she's the kind of friend it pays
to have," Mikey almost slugged her in the shoulder. "You don't have to *like* somebody to be her
friend," Margalo pointed out, and Mikey almost
slugged her on the back. Margalo was right and
Mikey knew it. But Mikey didn't know how to
make Margalo see how wrong that right was.
Except maybe by slamming a math workbook
down on Margalo's head, which she did. But when
she did that, Margalo just smiled, like a cat with
canary feathers sticking out of its mouth, and said,
"Hitting me with a math workbook doesn't prove
anything."

Mikey didn't know how she felt about Linny
not being at this, her first slumber party. Ronnie
Caselli was there, so it wasn't a party only losers
were going to be at, and Tanisha Harris, also ma-
jorly popular, and Mikey personally didn't mind either one of those two. Ronnie and Tanisha would
make things okay, even if there were two strangers
— African-Americans, probably from Doucelle's
church, church friends — and strangers always
took a while to stop disliking Mikey. Lizzie and

Coral, Doucelle introduced the church friends to everybody. Lizzie and Coral stuck pretty close. Mikey was sticking close to Margalo, herself.

Surprise two was the new girl, Gianette St. Etienne, if you could believe that was anybody's real name, which Mikey personally didn't. The new girl had started school a week late and she came late to this party, too. When she entered, they were all sitting around on the floor in the family room, sleeping bags and pillows in a big pile against one wall, the sliding patio doors opened to the warm afternoon air, watching Doucelle open presents. Mikey was sitting back against a wall, alone, pretty bored so far, half wishing she'd refused the invitation. Then Gianette St. Etienne — whose name was as dark and exotic as her curly hair — came in, looking unlike everybody else. Everybody else wore jeans and T-shirts, sneakers, while she wore a twirly skirt and a puffy-sleeved cotton blouse. Everybody else looked like they were starting to turn into teenagers, but Gianette was tiny and flat-chested, with big dark cocker-spaniel eyes, like some doll who had been magicked alive.

The differences went deeper, too. Everybody else had families that made some kind of sense, fathers and mothers, divorced or not, stepparents and their families mixed in, parents with jobs that made sense. Even Tanisha, who was adopted, along with her adopted brothers and sisters, had a normal family. Not Gianette. Gianette had no parents left, with a dead father and a disappeared mother. She had been sent to Newtown to live with her grandmother, "A *belle-dame*," Gianette told them, the first day she came to school, telling the circle of girls all about herself. "This is what we Creoles call a witch woman. I can't really splain it to you." She had already told them she couldn't say the letter *x*.

Mikey didn't believe a word of it, and neither did Margalo. Everyone else did, though, so Margalo kept her mouth shut and watched. That left only Mikey to be sarcastic, about the *belle-dame*, and the Creole, too. "Did she say Crayola? She's a Crayola?" Mikey asked, and got shushed.

The reason Gianette couldn't pronounce *x*es had also to do with being Creole, from New Orleans, Louisiana, where there was a lot of French, a language in which — as everyone knew — the *x*s were silent. Her Creole, *belle-dame*, witch grandmother was teaching Gianette magic spells, and how to grow herbs and poisons along with vegetables in the garden of the house they rented, a solitary house, at the entry gates to the long, overgrown driveway belonging to an abandoned mansion. Haunted, Gianette claimed. "I spect my granny keeps those ghosts trapped inside that old house," Gianette told them. "She's a ghost driver, too."

"Like I believe in ghosts," Mikey said, and got shushed.

There was something about Gianette that people liked. She always had a little smile on her face as if she knew a secret, and if you asked her the right way, she'd tell you. All of the boys had crushes on her. Even Louis Caselli, who had the personal charm of a warthog, hoped to attract her attention. There was definitely something about Gianette, and when that something got added to Doucelle's slumber party, everything got more exciting. Nothing changed, but everybody felt that somebody special had come to the party.

Mikey drew her knees in against her chest and scowled. Margalo frowned at her. "What's your problem?" Mikey muttered. "Have you turned into my mother?"

Gianette didn't say a word. She just sat down, in the middle of her skirt.

Everybody watched her.

Gianette smiled to herself.

Mikey thought that after about five more

seconds of this, she'd slam a pillow right at that smiling face.

Gianette asked, "What have you been given, Doucelle?" and everybody came out of the trance.

Doucelle showed her the little silver cross from Coral, and the earrings Lizzie had made out of glittery beads; and Gianette asked Lizzie to make her a pair of earrings too. There were the two tapes, from Margalo and Mikey, a red bandanna for a head scarf from Tanisha, and Ronnie had offered a gift certificate from the bookstore at the mall. Denise had found a pair of silver shoelaces, which Doucelle had just unwrapped and exclaimed over. Gianette agreed about those. "An escellent accessory."

"Accessory?" Mikey muttered to Margalo in mock amazement. "I thought they were shoelaces."

Doucelle reached out for the present Gianette offered her. It was wrapped in cloth. When Doucelle unwrapped it, the present looked like a clump of straw.

"A doll?" she asked, trying to sound pleased. "What a — How nice, Gianette, a straw doll. Thank you," Doucelle said, all politeness. The doll was about four inches tall, straw with cloth stapled around it for clothes, and black blotches of ink for eyes.

"It's Frankenstein's baby!" Mikey cried.

Gianette laughed, a little fake tinkly laugh, like one of those tiny cheap souvenir china bells you can buy in tourist shops. "Not a doll, no, let me splain, you don't know. I didn't spect you would understand — my granny made this. Special for you, Doucelle. A doll made by a *belle-dame*," Gianette said, giving the word three soft and sinister syllables, *bell-eh-dahm*. "This will keep you safe, safest of all, safe forever. No harm can come to you, however much ill anyone wishes you, when you have the *belle-dame*'s doll. You must keep it under your mattress, at the zact center. Can you do that?"

"Of course. Do you want to see my room?"

Gianette wasn't sure, but she allowed herself to be persuaded. Denise went with them, because she was the best friend, and Ronnie said she was always curious about people's rooms, so she trooped along too. Doucelle said, "You can help me get the doll in the right place, Gianette."

"My granny put all the good spells on this doll, so nobody can ill-wish you, and for a passionate, rich husband, too."

"And handsome?" Denise added.

"Yes, but," Gianette turned, so that she was saying this to everyone, including Coral and Lizzie, who were rising to join the crowd. "All men are handsome. Only women can be bad to look at." Her smile included Mikey and Margalo. "Ugly or fat or clumsy, or bony like a chicken."

Mikey smiled right back at Gianette, all teeth.

"Can I have a doll like Doucelle's?" Denise was asking as they left the room, and Gianette was answering, "Yes, escept it isn't a gift, so you must cross my palm for it, or the *belle-dame*'s spells won't stick." Coral asked, "How much? Because I want one too," and so did Lizzie, and Gianette was the last of the line of girls leaving the room, saying "Ten dollars, perhaps twenty, my granny decides for each one how much magic is required, how many spells."

This left Mikey and Margalo with Tanisha Harris, left behind in the family room of Doucelle's house. Tanisha was tall, long-legged, and looked like a swimmer although in fact she planned to make her mark in volleyball. Tanisha lounged back against a pile of sleeping bags, not impressed by Gianette. Not much impressed Tanisha, and nothing rattled her. If Tan didn't feel left behind here, Mikey wasn't going to either.

"At twenty dollars a doll," Margalo said, "you could make a lot of money. Even at ten dollars you could. If people believed in magic dolls."

"Gullah superstition," Tanisha said. "That's what my folks would call it. That, and the numbers, and now the lottery, too, they're the ruination of my people," she declared.

"Don't forget drugs and welfare," Margalo reminded her.

Tanisha sat up straight, and grinned. "Maybe you should try some Gullah magic on your folks," she suggested to Mikey. "Maybe there's a love potion that would keep them together?"

"I'd rather buy some poison off this granny *belle-dame*," Mikey answered. And why was Margalo giving her the eye like that? "Did you know she was going to be here?" she demanded of Margalo.

"No, but I would have guessed. Are you going to leave?" Margalo asked Mikey.

"Do you want to?" Mikey asked Margalo.

Margalo just shrugged, as if she didn't care about anything.

"Doucelle said we're having hamburgers," Tanisha said. "It's been a while since I've had a good hamburger." Tanisha went to look out the sliding glass door. Mr. Scott was one of those fathers who wore a cooking apron when he grilled. "Think they'll toast the buns?"

"My mother has cut out high-fat foods," Mikey

told Tanisha. Margalo already knew this. "I'd hate to miss out on hamburgers."

"My family is vegetarian. Except for me," Tanisha said.

Margalo laughed at that, because, as she told them, "*We* can't afford the meat for hamburgers for everyone."

"So you aren't leaving," Tanisha said. "Good."

There were the three of them, at least, Mikey thought. How bad could it get, if there were three of them?

They sat together at the supper table, for hamburgers and chips, with Pepsi and root beer to choose between. They joined in the conversation about schools, and TV shows, and the dumb habits their families had. Margalo told a couple of Weird Esther stories, ending with Weird Esther and her bodiless doll. Esther kept the bodiless doll's head on her pillow, "One of those blond heads where the hair comes out in bunches, out of round holes in straight rows," Margalo told them. "She names it after whoever she likes best. It was me for a while," Margalo told them, "when Aurora first married their father. Now it's Mikey." Ronnie sort of complained and sort of boasted about being the only girl in a bunch of brothers, with only two girl cousins. "Boys have stinky feet, they all do,"

Ronnie said. "Does anyone know why?"

"Try being an only child," said Mikey, putting together a mouthful of cake topped with both frosting and ice cream. "They have nothing to do but pay attention to me. Let me tell you, that's what Hell must be like." She hoped Lizzie and Coral, being church friends, might get upset by that word, but they didn't even notice. Mikey was disappointed in them.

"I really feel sorry for you, Mikey — your own room and bathroom, a big house, all those presents at Christmas," Tanisha said, sarcastic, but Denise said, with her way of making everything a question, "My mother says I should be grateful? To her, because I'm not an only child? Because she was?"

And Ronnie remarked, "Maybe that'll be a good thing about if your parents get divorced, Mikey. There'll be only half as many parents on your case."

"People don't have to stay divorced," Doucelle told them. "My aunt was only divorced for three months. It's true. But she had a good job and no children, so she got another husband right away. My parents are still married, but most aren't, isn't that true? Except yours, Tanisha, because you're adopted."

"Being adopted has nothing to do with staying married," Tanisha said.

"You are adopted? Do you know who your real parents are?" Gianette wondered.

"Mom and Pop are my real parents. You mean biological."

"I could ask the cards about them. You could have a reading to discover where they are now, and what kind of people they are."

"No thanks," Tanisha said. "If I want to know, I'll ask Mom and Pop."

"But what if there is some disease, in your blood? And it will strike you down?"

"Or better," Margalo said, "what if there's a huge fortune waiting for you to inherit it?"

"I could like that," Tanisha said. "That's a fantasy I could get into."

"If you were stolen from some wealthy family, when you were a baby," Margalo suggested.

"You mean, like, left in a box outside an orphanage?" Tanisha asked. "Except I came through an agency, straight from a hospital."

"Or kidnapped by a wicked uncle?" Denise said.

"It's *The Lion King*!" Mikey cried out, and everybody laughed. "Not funny," she said. "You should sue Disney for stealing your story. You could make millions. Think of it, Tan. What would you do with all that money?"

"Or if you won the lottery," Coral said.

"What would you get, if you won the lottery?" Doucelle asked everyone around the table. "What would we do with all that money?"

Mikey knew what she'd do: invest it in tax-free municipal bonds and become independent, self-supporting.

After she turned eighteen, of course, and she wouldn't give any to her parents, either. She could be just as selfish as them.

"I would buy the mansion, for the *belle-dame* to live in, and I would live there with her. She would drive out the ghosts and I would have it all fixed up — after the fire, it is much damaged — and I would make it as beautiful as it once was. My grandmother would live there, like the queen that she is."

"Making you a princess," Margalo said. Everybody sort of snickered, but Gianette didn't notice.

"But I already am," she answered.

"Like the book," Margalo said with a sideways look for Ronnie but not for Mikey, as if Mikey wouldn't get the reference.

Mikey got the reference, and got the insult, too. What was wrong with Margalo?

"You mean, that one they made the movie out of?" Coral said, and "I saw it," Denise said, and

Doucelle said, "It was a TV show, too," and the conversation switched to *Dr. Quinn*, because it was Saturday. Nobody wanted to miss *Dr. Quinn*, and Sully. Nobody except Mikey, that is, and Margalo, too, she knew; but neither of them said anything. Mikey figured it was so far, so good, for her at this slumber party, so why risk it?

The others flopped down in front of the TV set at eight, and Mikey went back into the kitchen, with Margalo and a pack of playing cards. Mr. and Mrs. Scott, with the impatient help of Richie — who had a party to get to, his friends were expecting him, it would be rude of him to be late and his parents never listened to him anyway, he didn't know why he bothered — had completely cleaned up the kitchen, after the party had finished eating. Now they were all either out or upstairs, all out of the way.

Mikey sat down at the kitchen table and shuffled the cards. "What do you want to play?" she asked Margalo, who said, "You told everybody. After you told me not to, and made me promise."

"I don't want to talk about it," Mikey said. She didn't, either. She didn't have to and nobody could make her.

"Why did you do that?"

"I couldn't not talk about it. Could I?"

"Who cares?" Margalo said.

"So why don't you just go watch *Dr.* stupid *Quinn* with everyone else?" Mikey demanded. "If I'm so bad."

"You know I hate that show," Margalo said.

"You didn't care anyway, you just told me you were busy having your dinner with your big happy family, and you never told me any of your ideas for me to do to stop them."

"Because I haven't thought of any," Margalo said, just as cross as Mikey. "You're always in such a hurry, as if everything is easy. Divorce isn't easy," she said.

"Tanisha said I can stay at her house if things get too bad for me," Mikey said. Who did Margalo think she was? Mikey's only friend? "Ronnie says divorce is hardest on the children, the way they just get tossed around."

Mikey knew what she wanted from Margalo, but it wasn't what she got. What she got was Margalo saying, "Yeah, well, maybe it is, but a bad marriage is hardest on the children too, if you want my opinion. If you want my opinion — "

"Well, I don't."

" — the way things work, whatever it is, it turns out to be hardest on the children. Like crack babies. Talk about underprivileged groups. Talk about the disadvantaged. Look at kids — no jobs, no income, no rights, except what rights our parents give us."

"Like the right to go to school?" Mikey was getting into this gripe session. "Say, there's a big right."

"The right not to be able to work until we're sixteen."

"The right not to vote. The right not to drive." Mikey had never really thought how bad things were for kids. "They can't do this to me," Mikey said.

"They can," Margalo told her. "And they do. Not Aurora," she said. "I can count on Aurora. I wish she'd adopt you, Mikey. But she can't, and she's outgrown her maternal phase anyway. She even had her tubes tied, because she said she's got all the children she can manage."

"I thought it was Steven who had the vasectomy."

"He did. They both had operations, because they couldn't decide which of them ought to be the one to do it."

"They really are a pair," Mikey said.

And, "Who are? What pair do you speak of? Why are you out here alone, do you have no other friends?" Gianette asked, swishing her skirt into the kitchen. She carried a flat box wrapped up in silver cloth. "No, don't splain, I also am bored. We'll read tarot. I have brought the cards," she said, and sat down at the table next to Mikey, unwrapping what turned out to be a thin deck of oversized cards.

Mikey exchanged a glance with Margalo. She knew what Margalo was thinking. Gianette gave them the pip, but if this was interesting — or stupid enough to be funny — they'd go along with it. For a while, at least, just to see what happened.

Gianette spread her cards out on the table without shuffling them. The backs were decorated with golden stars and silver crescent moons and comets with streaking tails, all on a blue background, like the night sky. Gianette kept pushing the cards around in a circle. She turned to look at Mikey. "You have a question," she announced, like some original-cast *Star Trek* alien priestess. "If you are right-handed, then you wash the cards with your left hand. So, you wash them — so — as I am — in a circle. As you do this, you think of your question. The cards will answer you."

Mikey looked across at Margalo.

Margalo rolled her eyes up under her eyelids. She raised her hands off the table, levitating them.

Mikey figured, probably Margalo thought that was how somebody hypnotized looked. She turned her attention back to Gianette's instructions.

"Put your left hand down, here. Good. Now, gently, let your hand wash the cards," Gianette repeated, an alien priestess playing a broken record.

Why not? Mikey thought, even if it was a stupid way to shuffle the cards. Are my parents going to get divorced? That would be her question. It was an inefficient way to shuffle, too, and Mikey would have been more comfortable riffling the cards, as she usually did. She thought, Are my parents going to get divorced?

Because if she knew the answer to that question, she could make some plans.

"Think only of your question, think only of that," Gianette said. She closed her eyes and tilted her head back.

The room got quiet, except for the swishing sound of the cards moving around on the tabletop, and the whispery sound of Gianette talking, telling them, "These cards are the Major Arcana of the ancient tarot pack, from ancient Egypt. When the time has come, you will turn over one card. One card only. And I will read the card for you. These are the cards the *belle-dame* has given to me, for my own use. I have made them mine and they speak to me. Through me, the cards will give you your true answer."

Are they going to get divorced? Mikey thought. Then she thought, This is stupid. Then she thought, It can't do any harm, can it? Then she thought, Are they going to do it?

She stopped moving the cards. And didn't look at Margalo.

"Now. Take up the card. You know which one it is. Lay it face up, facing up at you."

Gianette didn't sound at all like a sixth-grade girl. She sounded like she really had powers.

Mikey turned over a card.

Roman numeral XIII: thirteen. A skeleton, riding a white horse.

Lucky she wasn't superstitious, Mikey thought. Because thirteen combined with a grinning skull looked like bad news to her. Or at least Halloween.

She looked up to see Margalo watching her.

"Death," Gianette whispered.

Mikey laughed out loud. "Oops."

Gianette didn't seem to even hear Mikey's laughter. "Think of your question."

Well, of course Mikey could figure it out. The answer to her question was yes. Death sounded like a divorce to her. Unless someone was going to die in her family? She hoped it wasn't her.

"Death rides close by," Gianette told Mikey. She whispered, "I spect you are in grave danger."

"What do you mean?" Mikey demanded, not whispering a bit.

"Illness. Accident. There might be an enemy, a spell. If your parents' divorce is an ill-wishing spell upon *you*, you have a strong enemy."

"Who told *you*?" Mikey demanded. "How do you know about that?"

Gianette took a few seconds transforming herself from Gypsy fortune-teller into sixth grader. Then, "Who told me?" she asked in her normal voice, with a little secret smile that turned up the corners of her mouth. "I don't like to say," she said.

But Mikey knew who. "You *told*," she accused Margalo. "I thought I could trust you."

"Your question, it concerned the divorce?" Gianette asked.

"It doesn't matter," Mikey said. But it did.

"Nowadays everybody gets divorced," Gianette consoled her.

Mikey wanted to punch Gianette in the face. Or maybe a roundhouse punch to the ear. She didn't actually know what a roundhouse punch was, but it was the kind of name the punch she wanted to lay on the side of Gianette's smug little curly-haired head would have.

Gianette was too small to punch, though, so Mikey just stared into Gianette's big brown eyes and smiled. For just a second, Mikey felt as if Gianette was an enemy, a personal enemy, and her smile got wider, toothier.

"And now, Margalo, will you try your chance with the cards? Have you your own question?" Gianette asked, turning away from Mikey.

"Sure." Margalo glared at Mikey.

Probably Margalo's question was whether she had to go on being Mikey's friend. Margalo had other friends, so she didn't need Mikey. She was better at pretending to be nice than Mikey was; Mikey knew that. They both knew it. Mikey really stank at being nice.

Margalo pushed the cards around in circles, washing them, while Gianette did her alien-priestess-Gypsy-fortune-teller's-voice talk. When Margalo turned over a card, Gianette gave a little moaning sound. "The Tower! Oh, Margalo. A dangerous, sad card. The lightning prepares to strike!"

Margalo stared at the card and nodded her head just a little. Then she looked right at Mikey and crossed her eyes, so quickly that Mikey barely saw it. This was one of their signals, but Mikey couldn't tell what it meant.

"I regret that I offered you the cards, Mikey. Margalo too," Gianette said, gathering up her cards and wrapping them in the silver cloth, saying in her normal voice, as if she was saying something normal, "Two such bad readings . . . but I am only a beginner, and perhaps the cards are wrong," she said, with irritating mysteriousness. "I go now. I spect the others will want to ask their questions. But they will have to cross my palm with silver, to hear what the cards say."

"I don't have any money," Margalo said.

"It's too late, anyway," Mikey pointed out. "You already told us."

Gianette looked at them for a long time, then said, "I know that." She swished out of the room.

Mikey looked at Margalo. "Bummer," she said.

"Death and disaster," Margalo agreed.

They grinned at each other, uneasily.

4.

Now That's a Good Time

Mikey waited for Margalo to say something about being sorry for telling Mikey's secret.

Margalo didn't say anything.

Finally Mikey demanded, "What was *your* question?"

Margalo shook her head. "None of your business."

Why not? Mikey wanted to ask, but didn't. "You know what *my* question was," she pointed out.

"Not because you wanted me to know," Margalo pointed out.

"So what?" Mikey asked, but if Margalo had already told the secret, it was too late for fighting about that to do any good, so Mikey changed the subject. "Are all slumber parties like this? Is this all that happens? Because it hasn't been much fun so far."

Margalo didn't want to be fighting either, even if Mikey had blamed her for something she hadn't done. "After the parents go to bed," she said, "sometimes we call in phone dedications. You could dedicate a song to Louis. If he was listening, he'd hate it."

Mikey said, "That's not fun, that's stupid. And then everybody giggles — they do, don't they? — when the deejay announces it."

"Because it's funny," Margalo said.

Mikey had her own opinion about that, but she was here at this slumber party, so she might as well try to enjoy herself. "What time do the parents usually go to bed?" she asked, still thinking about telephones. "We could dial an overseas number. Have you ever talked to someone who doesn't speak English? And the time zone would be different too. Want to?"

Margalo's eyes lit up. "We could pretend it's a wrong number. They don't charge for wrong numbers on long distance, do they? As long as you call up and report it, I think there's a law about that. What about Japan?" she asked. "Want to try Japan? Do you think they say 'Hello' in Japan, like the French say *'Allô'*?"

"Why not Spain?" There was actually an educational reason for calling Spain, because when Mikey got to high school, she might take Spanish.

"Because," Margalo said. "Just because. But Mikey, do you think Gianette really knows how to do a tarot reading?"

"Ask me if I think cardboard rectangles with weird pictures on them can know anything about my life," Mikey answered. "Ask me what I think about astrology. You mean you really didn't tell her? About my parents?"

"I told you, I didn't. Who did *you* tell? Besides me, I mean, because I know I didn't tell anyone, whether you believe me or not. Because you told me it was such a big secret."

"I said I was sorry," Mikey said.

"No you didn't."

"That's because I'm not."

Margalo got up from the table, then, and walked out of the kitchen.

Mikey got up too, but she stayed stomping around the kitchen for a few minutes. Somebody had told her secret, as if it was gossip. She couldn't figure out who it would have been, Ronnie or Tanisha, because she knew Margalo lied but not to her. Mikey couldn't think of how to get even with whoever told, either, especially since it was sort of her own fault. Mikey stomped out of the kitchen and back into the family room, where the slumber party had turned off the TV. They were doing hair. They were combing and braiding, mousseing and styling. Somebody had even brought an electric curler in her overnight case. That somebody even *owned* an electric curler alarmed Mikey. Margalo was making a long skinny braid, starting at the top of her head. Next to her, Lizzie was doing the same thing, with her shorter, thicker, wiry hair. "We're going to wrap them," Margalo greeted Mikey. "Lizzie brought lots of thread. You want to have a wrap too?"

It was all even more stupid than Mikey had ever imagined. She fiddled with the radio for a while, until everybody yelled at her, then she read *TV Guide* just to pass the time. Gianette let Doucelle pile her curly hair on top of her head and pin it up there like some *Playboy* model, except that all the rest of her was so flat and straight and childlike, looking at her gave Mikey fits. When

Gianette saw Mikey having fits at her, she asked, "Did you like your tarot reading?" so everyone asked Mikey what Gianette meant. After that, everybody wanted to have her cards read.

Gianette insisted on setting a scene before she would do anything. Doucelle turned down the lights. Nobody could play any music while Gianette told fortunes, or turn on the TV. Everybody would have to cross her palm with silver, or a dollar if they didn't have any quarters. Gianette was turning herself into the queen of the slumber party. So Mikey suggested that they go out back and burn squares of to

"I know how," she said.

But Doucelle wanted to have fortunes told. Gianette said people could take turns coming inside for their fortunes. Doucelle said she had promised her parents they wouldn't be any trouble. Tanisha said they could stay on the blacktop, on the driveway, and she for one promised not to scream if she got burned. Doucelle said she didn't know where her father put the matches anyway, and Mikey said she'd look for them.

"It's perfectly safe," Mikey assured them all, even though she had no idea if that was true or not, and didn't care. How much harm could a burning square of toilet paper do, anyway?

"You wouldn't," they said to her, except Margalo. Everybody except Margalo agreed, "You wouldn't dare."

Leading a pack of girls out to the dark backyard to find the box of kitchen matches by the barbecue, going back inside to take the roll of toilet paper from its holder in the downstairs bathroom, getting ready to play with matches, play with fire, Mikey thought maybe slumber parties weren't so bad after all. She thought maybe she'd like it if she got invited to another one.

But Doucelle told them it was time for *Saturday Night Live*, so they all went back to the family room, turned up the lights, and turned on the TV. "We can watch it, but we have to keep the volume down," Doucelle warned them. "My parents don't approve of it."

Neither did Ronnie's ("My mom says it's degrading and vulgar — but she's still living in the fifties") nor Coral's ("They say it's really gone downhill since the first two years"), but Margalo volunteered that "Aurora and Steven like it. They always watch if they can, and so can we if we're up."

"Wait a minute," Tanisha said. "Let me get this straight. The same people who won't let you watch the six o'clock news join you in watching *Saturday Night Live*?"

"Actually, *I* join *them*," Margalo said.

"Does that make sense to you?" Denise asked Margalo.

"Sure, perfect sense."

"Why do you not call your mother 'Mother'?" Gianette asked, but somebody else said, "I thought your mother was waging a world war against television," and Lizzie bet her parents would like *SNL* too, if they'd ever watch it, and Margalo said, "It's only as long as there are kids under ten still awake that she cares."

"Half the time your parents are real space cadets," Mikey announced, "but I agree with them about TV."

"Did she tell you to call her by her name?" Gianette asked. "Or was it your idea?"

"If you think about it," Mikey addressed the group. "Here are these kids — us, when we were little, I know it happened to me, I can remember it. They'll spend the afternoon watching *Sesame Street*, *Mister Rogers*, Big Bird, and remember King Friday the Thirteenth? Then — *bam*! Right between the eyes! They're watching some film clips of massacres in Rwanda. With machetes, people dragged out of their houses. Or some plane wreck. Or some politician, who looks like a major criminal warlord — and everybody is terribly serious, worried. I mean, no wonder there are so many druggies and dropouts. How can a little kid take that kind of schizophrenia?"

Other people remembered that same experience, "and *we're* not psychopaths, so your theory doesn't always work," but Margalo asked them to be quiet so she could hear. Gianette said this might be her only chance ever to watch the show, since her grandmother didn't have a TV. Everybody settled down.

After *SNL* it was the deep of night, a thick, black silence inside the house and all around outside. It was so late and so dark that any sleepiness anyone might have been feeling disappeared. Completely. They split off into separate activities. Gianette read the cards for Coral, and Doucelle, and Denise, a full reading, she said, and she didn't charge as much as many other querents would because she knew she was still a beginner. Although the *belle-dame* said she was gifted. "I have a gift," Gianette told them, "so you are fortunate in me."

Only Margalo and Tanisha and Ronnie went outside with Mikey. Lizzie was going to go with them, until she realized that Mikey meant to do exactly what she said. "Fire's dangerous," Lizzie said.

Duuhh, Mikey thought, but all she said out

loud — since she wanted to continue enjoying the party, if she could, and not make any new enemies, if she could avoid it — was "This isn't dangerous. Not if you're careful."

Lizzie shook her head and backed from the kitchen into the family room, where Gianette had candles burning on the center of the coffee table and the lights turned off.

"Wait'll you see," Mikey promised the remaining three.

Outside there were streetlights, but mostly there was night, and the hulking shapes of houses sitting on their lawns at the ends of pale sidewalks, guarded by their dark-leaved trees. "No moon," Mikey observed. "That's good." She was whispering.

They all whispered, meaningless conversation, just words, "Dark," and "Late," and "What — ?"

"No wind, not to speak of," Mikey whispered. "That's good," she whispered as they stood on the paved driveway. No lights showed behind the front windows of Doucelle's house.

A car motor broke the silence. They all waited, not moving. Was it coming closer? Down the street by this house? Would the headlights catch them — like wild animals frozen in the bright glare of headlights? Should they hide? Where could they — But the car stayed at a distance, until it drove out of earshot.

"Okay," Mikey said. She took off a square of toilet paper and passed the roll to Margalo. She pinched the center of the square between three fingers, as if she planned to make a paper flower out of it. Holding the pinched square and the matchbox in one hand, she struck a match and dropped the matchbox.

Even Mikey didn't want to see what would happen if you lit a whole box of kitchen matches at one time.

When she held the match to it, flame caught at the edges of the square, just a brief red-hot line, and then — the paper caught fire.

Mikey let it go. For half a second, maybe a second and a half, the flame floated down on dark air. A flame leaf, or an opened hand of flame, sank slowly through air as black as deep water. When it landed, it burned blue, then red as coals, and it disappeared into darkness.

"All *right*," Margalo said.

"Neat," Ronnie said.

"Let me try," Tanisha said.

For a while they lit the little paper squares and set them sailing on the dark night air. Sometimes they lit just one, sometimes all four as close to simultaneously as they could get the matchbox passed around. Sometimes they spaced them — counting to four between — so that there would be a continuous flow of flame, floating like a river of light.

When the box of matches ran out, they still didn't want to go inside. Outside was where adventures might happen, in the shadows surrounding trees, and hedges, buildings. When a car drove down Doucelle's street, Mikey's stomach got cold, then cinched in as tight as if by a belt.

She couldn't imagine what might happen, and she knew nothing was going to happen, but outside, in the night, anything could happen.

No wonder people liked slumber parties. You were practically free.

But they couldn't think of any excuse to stay outside, so they picked up all the matches they could find by feeling around on the blacktop — and that was a lot of matches — returned what was left of the roll of toilet paper, and went into the kitchen. To see who was there and what was up. To eat potato chips and think of more ways to stay awake.

"We could stay up all night," Mikey said as they went into the family room. She carried a bag of chips, and Ronnie had pretzels.

"Why would you want to do that?" Gianette greeted them.

Coral, and Doucelle, and Denise were all three looking smirky on the sofa. Mikey didn't care about their secrets. They couldn't possibly have interesting secrets.

"Have you been hearing about tall, dark, handsome strangers coming to carry you off?" Margalo asked them.

"And rich," Coral added.

"Rich," Gianette explained, with a little smile, "matters more than we think it does when we are falling in love. My mother has splained this to me, many times."

"I don't agree," Tanisha said. "I don't plan for anyone ever to support me. I plan to look out for myself."

"No, no. If your husband is rich, then you can never be left without means," Gianette explained. "You can't be abandoned."

Denise, whose divorced father hadn't been to see her since third grade, pointed out, "You can always be abandoned, whether you're rich or not. Money just means you don't have to worry about being homeless."

"I'm glad my family's Catholic," Ronnie said.

"Why?"

"Because Catholics can't get divorced."

"Yes they can," Doucelle said. "My uncle Jonas married a woman who's Catholic — because they had to raise their children Catholic — and Aunt Cecile was divorced. She's the one he married."

"Okay, sometimes they can, but it's much, much harder. And they don't want to, because after that they can't be married by a priest, so they're not married in the eyes of the Church. I asked my mother. Except for Catholics, everybody can get divorced. In America, anyway, I don't know about Iran or China. In America at least, all you have to do is figure out about child support, if there are children. My mother has a friend who — "

"Talk much about divorce, do you?" Mikey asked Ronnie, with an unfriendly smile.

"Not — " Ronnie said. Then, "Oh," she said. "But — I'm sorry," Ronnie said. "Only Linny."

"Right," Mikey answered. "Right," in her most sarcastic voice. "Thanks a lot," she said, with her wolf smile.

"Really sorry, Mikey," Ronnie said.

"So, do we want to try to stay up all night?" Tanisha asked quickly, and Mikey suspected that Tanisha, also, had told someone. But Margalo hadn't told, not anyone.

"My parents said we can stay up as long as we want to as long as we're quiet," Doucelle told them. "But I always fall asleep. I can't help it."

Gianette said, "Why should we want to keep ourselves awake, when we don't need to? Don't you agree?"

"I have to sing in the choir tomorrow," Lizzie reminded them. "And so do you, Doucelle. We can't be too tired to sing."

"Let's just see what happens," Ronnie said. "We don't have to *decide* what's going to happen. Do we? Can't we just relax?"

They changed into the extra-large T-shirts they had brought for sleeping in, spread out their sleeping bags, and lay down inside them. They left one lamp on, on the table beside the sofa, until Doucelle (who was sleeping on the sofa because it was her party) reached up and turned it off. At first people talked to everyone, and everyone talked. Then people talked in soft voices just to the people near them. After a while Mikey heard the voices getting thicker, slower, growing drowsy. Then there was the silence of eight people breathing in a dark room.

A voice whispered, "Mikey?"

"Margalo?" Mikey answered.

"No, Ronnie. You want to know something?"

"No," Mikey answered. She was still angry at Ronnie, but "Yes," Margalo whispered close beside her head, and Tanisha's voice whispered, "Just spit it out."

"I've got firecrackers."

They were all silent.

"And a box of matches."

When Mikey spoke again, it was in the lightest, most soundless voice she could find. "Let's go outside."

Nobody moved.

Everybody listened, to be certain that the other four party guests were slumbering.

Then they rustled out of their sleeping bags, and Tanisha protested, in a small, thin voice, "I can't find my clothes."

"It's dark outside. It's warm enough," Mikey said. "I don't plan to get dressed." She crept out of the room, silent as any movie Indian, or movie Indian scout, barefooted. She led them through the kitchen, and then out the front door, before she turned on Ronnie. "Why didn't you tell me?"

Ronnie ignored her. In the dim light from the corner streetlight she showed them a handful of long-stemmed firecrackers. "See? Actually, these belong to Louis and Sal, left over from the Fourth. I found them. In this not very secret hiding place they've built, under Sal's back steps."

"They're small," Mikey complained.

"They're illegal," Margalo pointed out.

"We can't set them off here," Tanisha announced.

"What?"

"Why not?"

"You afraid?"

"No, dummies. But it's the middle of the night. It must be two or maybe even three in the morning. People are bound to wake up, or at least I hope they will. But I'm not interested in getting into the kind of trouble we'll be in if we're caught. Are you?" Tanisha demanded.

"What if," Ronnie suggested, "we go down the street?"

Mikey was ready to move, but Tanisha had another objection. "I don't plan to go wandering along any streets dressed like this. At night. No neighborhood is safe if you go around behaving like a jerk. No matter how afflu-*ent* it is. And besides, didn't you hear about those girls?"

"The ones who got run over? I did," Margalo said.

"What girls?"

"They were at a slumber party," Margalo said. "In Wisconsin?"

"Or Minnesota, someplace like that. Iowa," Tanisha said.

Mikey was getting impatient just standing around, and her feet were getting cold too. Not that she was getting cold feet, just that it wasn't comfortable, standing on the blacktop without moving. "I don't care where — what happened? What does it have to do with us? Did they have firecrackers?"

"They were at a slumber party," Tanisha explained. "They snuck out to meet one of their's boyfriend."

"But none of us have boyfriends," Mikey pointed out.

"And three of them were killed by a hit-and-run driver," Margalo finished.

Mikey couldn't think of anything to say about that.

"That's so sad," Ronnie said. "It's — Did they catch the driver?"

"It was on the radio," Margalo added.

"Not the six o'clock news," Mikey said.

"How old were they?" Ronnie asked.

"Twelve, thirteen. Our age." Tanisha let that sink in. Then, "But I've got an idea," she said.

"We could go back inside, go to sleep," Ronnie suggested.

"The backyard," Mikey guessed. "But somebody else's backyard, not Doucelle's."

"Good idea," Margalo said, and "How will we get back in the house?" Ronnie asked.

"The sliding door's not locked, the one in the family room," Mikey told them.

They stood in dim and shadowy light. Their faces looked pale, with big eyes, except for Tanisha, whose face looked dark, with big eyes. Then Mikey grinned. Just grinned, because what if they really did it, set off firecrackers in the middle of the night in this well-behaved suburban neighborhood? What would happen if they did that?

"Let's do it," she said. It was the best idea she'd heard in weeks. "They can't catch us if we make sure we know our escape route before we set any off. Like the guy who survived the storm on Everest — he said he thought part of the reason was because he was careful to memorize the terrain ahead of time."

"Besides, we're only minors, and it's only mischief," Margalo said.

"Who says we'll get caught?" Tanisha asked. She led them around behind the garage, across the grass of the Scotts' backyard, across the neighbor's yard, and then up against a shoulder-high hedge. "Which way from here? Any ideas?"

Their feet whispered across dark, soft grass, grown thick and cut even. A dog barked, twice. Fell silent.

They waited, then moved on. They moved so quietly now, so wordlessly, even dogs couldn't hear them. The whole neighborhood slept.

'Twas the night before Christmas, Mikey thought, and was in danger of bursting out laughing. But there was that feeling in the dark air.

"Here," Tanisha said, at the trunk of a tree, big enough for one or two girls to crouch behind and hide. Even without any light, the leaves cast a denser darkness onto the ground. They faced each other, hidden in shadows.

Ronnie handed out the sticks. "I checked. They all have fuses. They should all work."

"What kind are they?" Mikey asked. "Cherry bombs?" she hoped.

"Rockets. Whistling moon rockets, and they really do whistle. Can you find the fuses? Just below the — "

"I've got it," Margalo said.

Mikey decided, "I'll go first. Give me the matches."

Ronnie didn't object — and that made everything even again between them, and okay again. Mikey hunkered down close to the ground, struck a match, and, by its light, quickly located the fuse end, flat against the long stick. Holding on to the bottom of the stick, she set the match beside the end of the fuse.

The fuse caught. It hissed, a quick *sss* sound; then the stick leaped out of Mikey's hand. The cracker took off, flew off the end of the stick, off and whistling. The whistle was high, piercing, like rockets in war movies. Then, before it was finished whistling, there was a *crack*! and explosion, like a car backfiring, or a gun going off.

Dogs broke out barking, all at once.

Then they broke out into silence, all at once, to listen.

The girls had their hands jammed across their mouths to muffle their laughter.

"Me, my turn," Ronnie said. She set off her own firecracker.

Margalo followed, then Tanisha, and by that time a couple of second-story windows were lit up.

"Okay, all the rest at the same time," Mikey said, General Mikey, thinking fast, acting fast. "As quick as we can, because once they start waking up . . . Get the rockets all ready and set out; we'll pass the matches back and forth. Then we make a break for Doucelle's. First to the hedge," she gave them their orders, and they listened. "Then slowly, creeping — no running across open yards — keep going to Doucelle's. First person there opens the door for the rest, okay?"

Nobody said anything.

"Everybody got it? Everybody ready?" Mikey asked. She had to make sure they had all heard the instructions. She couldn't see anybody's face, just the light shadows of T-shirts and two balloonlike bobbing pale faces. Tanisha was lucky.

"Well? Are you?"

"Yes. Absolutely," came the answer.

Mikey's troops awaited her next move. She told Ronnie to pass out the firecrackers, and Mikey lit the first match, then handed the box to Margalo before she touched the flame to the fuse. Margalo lit her match and handed off the box to Tanisha, like a relay-race runner, and it went on to Ronnie, then back to Mikey, for another round of whistling, popping firecrackers, one after the other, breaking the dark silence up with a commotion of noise.

Windows flew up. A man's voice called out: "What the devil's going on? Who's out there?"

Mikey's knees felt weak with laughter. "Shhh,"

she told the others. "Two more," Ronnie said. She struck a match, lit one fuse, and Mikey lit the last. The first rocket whistled. The second whistled. Then they exploded, *crack! crack!* Like pistols.

"Now!" Mikey set off, bent low and running. She led them back from the tree, across a lawn, then low by the hedge, invisible, she hoped, to the two men who were yelling back and forth out of their windows.

"You see anybody?"

"Damned kids."

"You sure it's kids?"

Mikey led everyone across a dark open patch of grass, low and slow to not make ripples across the darkness.

"I'm calling the cops."

"It's only kids."

Mikey's heart was racing as they headed for Doucelle's house. She felt — alive — excited — almost as if bullets and bombs might at any time explode around her. As if there was real danger.

They approached the sliding glass door, slow and sneaky. They snaked up to the door, but before Mikey could put a hand out to move it, the door opened enough to let them slip through, one at a time.

Gianette had been waiting for them.

Nobody said a word to her until they were all back in their sleeping bags.

"The others never woke," Gianette's voice said. "I spect they have no clue. Listen," she told them.

In the distance they heard police sirens. The sirens wound and wailed through the night outside the Scotts' house, where the slumber party lay on the floor in sleeping bags.

Mikey jammed her fist into her mouth, tucked her head down against her chest, and buried herself in her sleeping bag. When she could trust herself, she stuck her head out again. "Margalo?"

"Yeah, what?"

"That was fun. Ronnie?"

"Yeah?"

"That was a great idea."

It had been a while since Mikey had felt so good about things. She was too excited to go to sleep now. Outside, a bluish light pulsed dimly, from down the block in front of somebody else's house. Nobody in the family room said anything, not the sleeping people or the waking people. Mikey could hear some of the others falling asleep, until every-body but her, she was sure of it, was unconscious.

Everyone but her and Margalo, as it turned out. "Mikey?"

"What?"

"Why did you tell them?"

Mikey didn't need to ask who *they* were, or what they'd been told. She didn't need to talk about it, either.

"Mikey? When you said it was a secret."

"Just shut up," Mikey said.

She listened, and waited, but Margalo didn't say anything else.

But Margalo always had more to say.

Uh-oh, Mikey thought, feeling warm, drowsy. Then she remembered the sound of sirens, wailing, and she remembered running across the dark yards, and she fell asleep smiling.

5.
Can a Leopard Change Her Spots?

Margalo waited for Mikey to figure it out.

At first Mikey didn't notice anything. Mrs. Scott got them up at ten thirty. She had made pancakes for breakfast, with real maple syrup, and sausage links. They all sat around the kitchen table in their T-shirts, eating and talking. At first Mikey didn't even notice Margalo not even answering something as simple as "Did you ever try jam on pancakes?" But Mikey was busy being the heroine of the firecrackers, a secret heroine only the girls knew about, as if she was someone in the French Resistance, or the Underground Railroad. So Mikey didn't notice that Margalo stayed shut up at her all through breakfast.

She noticed but she didn't care while they were sitting around on Doucelle's front steps waiting for their mothers to pick them up. Margalo noted the expression on Mikey's round face, when for the third time Margalo didn't answer a question about how late Aurora was liable to be, picking up from a slumber party. The expression was irritated, mostly. Mikey wasn't used to being ignored.

Margalo knew that.

Margalo ignored Mikey and joined in on the conversation about how Gianette was getting home. At first Gianette was going to walk all the way home, but Mrs. Scott gave her enough money to take the bus. Ronnie's mother would drop her off by the bus stop in front of the Rite-Aid, and Gianette was describing the long bus ride out of town, and the trailer park she would get off at, before walking home down a deserted road between woods and fields. In this trailer park people tied their dogs up outside, using chains attached to stakes in the ground. "They leave them there all day and all night, too, to keep thieves away," she told the listening girls, and smoothed her skirt over her knees, and smiled a little sadly. "The dogs are not friendly, not even to me."

"Hunnh," Mikey snorted.

Margalo knew exactly what that snort meant, but she pretended she hadn't heard a thing. She didn't say a thing. Not even when Mikey's elbow dug into her ribs.

"One trailer — I don't know who lives there — I've never seen anyone around it when I have been waiting for the bus to come — there is a fox."

"You mean," Coral asked, "like a live fox? That's terrible! Tied up?"

"Why would they want a fox?" Margalo asked, and "That's cool," Tanisha said, and "Does it eat dog food? Or what?" Denise wondered, and Mikey suggested, "Maybe they plan to sell its fur. Doesn't your grandmother have a fur piece, Margalo? Mine does."

Margalo didn't say anything.

"Poor fox," Doucelle said, and Lizzie agreed, "We should call the ASPCA."

"Do you think it's against the law?" Mikey asked Margalo, who stayed shut up. "Is the ASPCA for wild animals, too?" she asked, staring right into Margalo's eyes, and didn't seem surprised when she got a silent no-answer from Margalo. "Boy, you *are* tired," Mikey said to Margalo, then added — as if Margalo had asked — "I'm not."

Doucelle told Margalo, "My mom says it's the day after the day you stay up late that you really feel bad. That's when you feel it, she says. So we should all be dragging at school tomorrow."

Margalo told Doucelle, "I'll take a short nap when I get home." Tanisha was listening too, and Ronnie. "Aurora says it's like traveling across time zones, like if you go to Europe. If you take a nap when you get there, even just for an hour, then you're right back your correct biological clock. In your right biorhythm."

Margalo didn't look at Mikey as she told people this.

"I'd rather sleep through school," Mikey said. "Wouldn't you, Margalo?"

Margalo stayed shut up.

And Mikey started to get it.

At first Mikey thought it was a game and she could win. Aurora picked them up, and Mikey sat in the back of the station wagon with Esther, behind Margalo. Margalo reported to her mother that it had been a good party and Aurora explained that Esther had begged to ride along and Mikey tried to trick Margalo into saying something to her. "We had tuna casserole for supper," Mikey said.

"Really," Aurora said, ready to believe anything, but Margalo wasn't going to fall for that trick.

"No," Mikey said, "really we had lobsters. Margalo loves lobsters, don't you, Margalo?"

"Really?" Aurora asked, slowing down for a turn.

Margalo happened to be looking hard, at something out her window.

"No, really we had hamburgers," Mikey said.

"That's nice," Aurora said.

"We never have hamburgers," Esther complained. "Do you like McDonald's? or Burger King best, Mikey?"

"I'll take either, doesn't matter to me, when I get a chance. You know how my mother feels about fast food," Mikey said.

"That grease isn't good for you," Aurora said. "Although I love Whoppers, myself."

"I thought it was the sodium," Mikey said. "Didn't you, Margalo?"

Margalo didn't answer.

"All the salt in fast food, that's what's really bad for you," Mikey said. "Margalo told me that, didn't you?" She waited for just a few seconds of silence before she explained, "See, Margalo isn't speaking to me."

Aurora wondered, "Did you two have a fight?"

"Not that I know of," Mikey answered.

Aurora looked over at Margalo, who smiled at her mother.

"I think she's having a nervous breakdown," Mikey suggested. "Or a split personality. Or hysterical muteness, unless — can amnesia make you forget how to talk?"

"Sometimes I think you'd give *me* a nervous breakdown," Aurora said to Mikey.

Margalo couldn't keep from practically laughing.

Mikey went on. "I don't know what's wrong with her. I think we should take her to the hospital. To the emergency room. For shots, shots with big needles."

"That's not a very kind suggestion," Aurora commented.

"Probably you told her to shut up," Esther suggested. "She does that to me sometimes. I really hate it. She's really good at it."

Margalo knew she was smirking, but she couldn't stop her face.

So Mikey told big lies about Margalo at the party, all the rest of the way until they arrived at her house. Both cars were gone from the garage.

"Will you be all right, alone?" Aurora asked.

"I like it better when they're not home," Mikey said. "Thanks for driving me. Talk to you later, Margalo," she said.

Margalo didn't say anything.

Margalo had just put the sleeping bag away in the attic when Susannah called her to the phone. Suspicious, she took it, but didn't say, "Hello?" She didn't say anything. She held the receiver to her ear and listened to the breathing.

"You're really being dumb," Mikey finally said.

Margalo stayed shut up.

"I have something interesting to say. Too bad for you."

It wasn't as if Margalo expected Mikey to apologize; she knew better than that. She knew Mikey thought every single thing she did was perfectly right and okay, so Mikey couldn't see any reason to ever apologize for anything.

Margalo never minded saying she was sorry. She knew everything *she* did wasn't perfect. She didn't even care if it was. She cared about getting what she wanted, or getting away with what she wanted, and apologizing often helped. But Mikey refused to be sorry about anything.

But that didn't mean Mikey could get away with telling Margalo to shut up, like some bug she was swatting. Margalo held on to the phone and didn't say anything.

"How long are you going to do this for?" Mikey demanded.

After a while Margalo heard Mikey slamming down her phone.

Monday, at school, the game went on. Sometimes Margalo almost couldn't stop herself from laughing, and sometimes Mikey looked like she was about to laugh too, which sort of changed the kind of game it was; and also Margalo wasn't sure just what would end it. If Mikey would say, *Okay, I shouldn't have told you to shut up and I won't again,* that would end it.

But that didn't sound like anything Mikey would say.

Margalo could tell that Mikey thought all she had to do was somehow trip Margalo up once, and then Margalo would stop staying shut up. How long could this go on? Margalo wondered as they ate their lunches side by side in the school's new cafeteria, with Mikey talking away and Margalo mute.

It wasn't easy for Margalo. There were things she wanted to say. For instance, she had her own opinions about Miss Brinson's reaction when she saw Joshua copying off David's math homework. Margalo didn't feel a bit sorry for the way David got yelled at. She didn't believe that Mikey really did, either; Mikey just liked arguing with teachers. Margalo would have liked to tell Mikey a few things about that, if she hadn't been shut up at her.

But when Miss Brinson kept Mikey in for the first ten minutes of soccer, that was different. Waiting in the bus line, Margalo saw Mikey come out from the meeting, and she wondered what Miss Brinson had said. Because Mikey looked about fifteen years old, or sixteen, and she wasn't even running, even though she had missed the start of practice.

Sitting in the back of the bus with Tanisha and Linny and Ronnie, Margalo decided to give up. What kind of a friend was it who kept on with some stupid shut-up contest, just to make her friend apologize for having said that, when the friend — that is, Mikey — was in some kind of trouble. They were all chattering away, and singing, and yelling at Howard and Clark up at the front seats, but Margalo was also thinking: She'd telephone Mikey and ask what Miss Brinson said, see if there was some way she could cheer Mikey up.

So when she had waited for Mikey to get home,

and called Mikey's number, she was looking forward to hearing Mikey be grateful.

"What do you want?" Mikey demanded.

If Mikey was going to be that way — "At least you could say thanks for calling?"

"Why should I?"

"You know what I mean," Margalo said.

"Now you can read my mind," Mikey said, sarcastic. "That sure saves me a lot of trouble."

"Never mind," Margalo said. "I'm sorry I called."

"So am I," Mikey agreed.

They both hung up.

Aurora was watching Margalo, and listening in on the conversation, at the same time as she was giving Lily a jelly sandwich, with the crusts cut off the bread. Aurora wore a wrinkled T-shirt; there were tomato-sauce stains on her front, because they were having spaghetti for dinner. Aurora had unruly hair and she didn't try very hard to get it to behave. "That Mikey," Margalo said to her mother.

"This is a hard time for her," Aurora said. "Will you get me a banana? and mash one for Lily? I didn't get any lunch."

"What do you mean?" Margalo asked, taking out a bowl and fork, reaching down two bananas from the top of the refrigerator.

"I had to take the little kids for shoes."

"No, about Mikey, about a hard time."

"With her parents getting divorced. No, sweetie, don't do that. Not you, Margalo." Aurora switched her attention back to Lily, to tell the little girl, "Margalo is making you your own special banana. With a spoon."

"Poon," Lily said happily.

"But first eat your sandwich," Aurora urged. "Good strawberry jelly." She peeled her own banana and ate it.

"Divorce wasn't hard on me," Margalo reminded her mother as she mashed Lily's banana with a fork.

"No sugar," Aurora reminded Margalo.

"Sugar," Lily protested.

"But how do you know — "

"Divorce was hard on Esther, you must remember that. I thought it was hard on you, too, I thought I remembered that, but — maybe I remember wrong."

"How do you know about Mikey's?"

"She told me." Aurora set the bowl and a spoon on the tray of Lily's highchair and sat down to watch Lily feed herself. Aurora watched her children eat the way some people watched sitcoms.

"Mikey told you?"

Aurora looked up. "Told me what? Did she have a good time at the party? You never said."

"Did Mikey tell you about her parents maybe getting divorced?"

"Why would Mikey tell *me*?" Aurora asked. "It was Patty. No thank you, sugar, Mommy doesn't want any. Would you dump the trash, sweetie?"

Margalo took the lid off the trash can. "Mrs. Elsinger told you? When?" Mrs. Elsinger had only just told Mikey, and Margalo didn't think the two mothers had been anywhere near each other since then.

"Last summer. One of the times she picked Mikey up here. Put a liner in, too, could you? Or we'll have banana all over the place. Patty said she'd postponed asking Anders for a divorce until school started, so Mikey would have school to distract her. How do you think the boys will feel about a vegetarian spaghetti sauce? Steven suggested that we eat one or two vegetarian meals a week. Isn't that a good idea?"

"Mrs. Elsinger knew last summer?"

"I have zucchini and onion, and some chopped green peppers," Aurora told her. "They won't notice. Not with cheese."

"Mrs. Elsinger must be serious about this," Margalo realized, and didn't expect an answer, which was lucky because she didn't get one. Instead, Aurora asked her if she would set the table, help get ready for supper.

"Or give Lily a bath. Baby? Do you want to take a bath with Margalo?"

"Yes!" Lily dropped her spoon, clapped her banana-coated palms, entirely happy.

Margalo wasn't a bit happy, not with Mikey, and not with Mrs. Lying Elsinger, and not even with herself — although that last one she really didn't understand.

She reminded herself that nobody could get away with shut-upping her, not even Mikey, not even if her parents *were* getting divorced.

But the next morning Mikey grabbed her arm when she was still on the steps of the bus, stepping down, and pulled her up the sidewalk into the school, and then hurried her into the library where they could talk privately, and said, "You have to tell me what you think. I know you've decided to talk to me."

Margalo figured that this was the nearest Mikey'd ever get to an apology. "Okay," Margalo said. "What's up?"

"Do you know why she called me in yesterday? Brinson?"

"No. How could I?"

"She told her. About the divorce. And Miss Brinson feels sorry for me. Now that she understands me."

Margalo tried to think of what to say. She thought. She couldn't think of anything. "Stupid," she said.

"Exactly," Mikey agreed. "Miss Brinson was — all about how many parents get divorced these days, so I don't have to be ashamed — she knows how hard it is on the children when parents get divorced — how she felt when her parents got divorced, even though she was much older, a senior in high school. On and on," Mikey complained. "As if I cared."

"Maybe that's not all bad," Margalo said. "Maybe she'll get you excused from music for a few weeks. You could cry a little — can you cry? You could ask her about music, if she feels sorry for you. You could say you need me with you, so I'd be excused too. We could get an extra free period every week that way."

"I'd rather miss art."

"But I *like* art," Margalo reminded Mikey.

"Art who?" Mikey joked, and they both groaned. Mikey showed her teeth in a smile.

Things were back to normal.

"Miss Brinson talked about how kids blame

themselves when parents break up. I told her I didn't and she told me it was only natural. She said if I had any worries I could always talk to her. Or questions. The only question I have is what my mother is up to telling my teacher that kind of stuff."

"Maybe to keep you from getting in trouble. When you blow up for no good reason?"

"There's always a good reason. No, what I want to know is what she's telling Miss Brinson for when she hasn't told me."

"She told Aurora, too."

"Your mother?"

"Last summer."

That got Mikey. Mikey stopped so still, Margalo couldn't hear her breathing, while anger pulsed out of her. Then Mikey frowned, the way she did over spelling lists, concentrating on something she hated and didn't care about, but had to do. Finally she asked, "Can you figure her out?"

Margalo shook her head.

"So everybody already knows. I guess. I guess the only person who thought it was a private secret was me. Miss Brinson kept telling me about books I could read and I finally told her, I don't need any books, what I need is different parents."

"What'll happen to you?" Margalo asked.

The library was starting to empty, which meant they didn't have much time left.

"They always used to say they couldn't get divorced because of me. I thought they meant it," Mikey said.

"Because they wanted to give you a home?" Margalo asked.

"Because neither one of them wants to be stuck alone with me," Mikey suggested.

"What'll you do?" Margalo asked.

"You're supposed to be figuring that out. *And* you've been refusing to say anything to me, just because you got into a snit."

Margalo was *not* going to apologize, not. Not when it was Mikey who had told *her* to shut up. No matter if Mikey's parents got divorced seven times, each one worse than the time before.

"And now you're getting into another one," Mikey said.

"Anyway, it takes a long time to get divorced," Margalo said. "You've got time."

"So I think I'll be perfect. I never tried that before. But you've got to help, Margalo. My mother will want to take me to the mall, you have to come too."

"Can you do that?"

"Go to the mall? It's not that har — "

"Be a perfect child. A perfect daughter."

"If you help, I can. I'm not stupid, I know what she wants."

The bell rang then, so Margalo only had time to reassure Mikey. "I'll think of things for you to do to act perfect."

She started a list during homeroom and added to it all morning. At lunch she presented it to Mikey. Mikey vetoed a few of the useless ideas. "Get excellent grades," for example, was on the list, until Mikey pointed out, "I already do." She also discarded a number of impossible ones, like, "Explain to Anders what it is that Patty doesn't like about him, so he can change what's wrong."

That suggestion started Mikey off, until she couldn't even swallow her lunch, she was laughing so hard. "I think I'll just buy them a copy of *The Joy of Sex*, what do you think?"

Gianette, whom Ronnie had moved over to make room for at the table, wanted to have "splained" to her what was so funny. Margalo answered, "The idea of giving advice to parents," but Gianette didn't get the joke, even when Margalo added, "About sex."

That cheered Margalo up too.

"My mother left me behind when I was a very little girl, almost unable to say my own name,"

Gianette told everyone else at the table.

"Add 'Get them to feel sorry for you,' " Margalo suggested to Mikey.

Mikey took the folded-up list out of her pocket and wrote that down. At that point people started asking, "Can we see the list?" but Mikey wasn't interested in sharing. The divorce had made her so popular — at least for the day — that nobody minded.

Margalo reached over to write the title that she had just thought of at the head of the list: MICHELLE ANGELA, in big letters for everyone to read.

Ronnie laughed, and so did Doucelle; then the others joined in.

It was a pretty good day, Margalo thought, and a good list, too:

1. Clean up bedroom.
2. Ask to go to the mall to shop for clothes.
   +Mo
3. Be taught how to cook meals.
4. Stop telling Mom when she's wrong.
5. Agree to baby-sit when Mom asks for her friends.
6. Ask Dad to do things — miniature golf, movies. +Mo
7. Let Dad give me tennis lessons.

8. Be pitiful.

(+Mo means: Margalo too.)

Margalo reached over to add 9. *Talk with Dad about his job.*

Mikey folded up the paper and put it into her pocket. "I'll let you know how it works out," she told Margalo, pretending she wasn't aware of everyone's attention.

"I have asked the *belle-dame* for a spell," Gianette said.

Mikey looked at her.

Gianette looked right back. A little smile picked up the ends of her mouth the way a girl might pick up her skirt to curtsey.

Mikey kept on looking.

Margalo watched this with interest.

"If the spell works, you will have to cross my palm," Gianette said. "With silver, or the spell will become reversed." She got up from the table.

"Wait for me?" Denise asked, rising, and half the table trailed off behind them, following Gianette out of the cafeteria.

"How about I cross your heart for you," Margalo asked Gianette's back. "Cross your street," Margalo said. "Cross your eyes. Cross your stitch."

"What?" Mikey asked. "What are you talking about? Has anyone ever told you how weird you are?"

"You," Margalo answered.

Now that they were alone at their end of the table, Mikey asked, "Have you thought of any way to stop the divorce?"

"Counseling. Marriage counseling. That's what Aurora did, with Esther and Howie's father. They went to a counselor, and it took a long time, three months. They were trying to iron things out. Because he had a girlfriend he was in love with but Esther and Howie didn't want to leave Aurora, because she was the only mother they had had, for years, because their mother had died. Did you think of that?"

"Killing my mother?" Mikey asked. "Yeah, a lot of times. But I'd never get away with it and I don't want to get myself locked up in jail until I'm thirty."

"You know what I mean," Margalo said. "But I don't know if yours would try counseling. I'm not sure they're the types. And it didn't work, anyway."

"Aren't you just as glad it didn't?"

"I wasn't at the time. When Aurora was married to him, we never worried about money."

The cafeteria was almost empty. The ladies came out to mop off the tables for the next lunch.

"Maybe, if my parents had to worry about money they wouldn't be able to get divorced. Maybe I should steal all their money."

"How would you do that?"

"You'd think of something. Don't you bet we could figure out a way?"

Margalo considered the question. She would have liked to answer yes, but she had a feeling that it wouldn't be as easy as it looked in movies. "Let's go outside," she said. "It's sunny."

"I'm serious," Mikey said. "Could we get ahold of their money?"

"I don't see how. I don't want to go to jail, either."

"We're juveniles," Mikey reminded her.

"No joke," Margalo said, and waited for Mikey to get it.

"Okay. But you still have to help me."

"I'm not cleaning up your room."

"I mean the mall. You have to. We'll have lunch in a restaurant. Not fast food," Mikey said. "And the movies. You like movies," Mikey told her, rising from the bench. "And you said you'd do miniature golf, so it's too late to back out. How about tennis? If I learn tennis, you should too, so I can beat you."

"I don't have a racquet."

"I think Mom does. You can use hers."

"I'm unathletic."

"We can't help that."

"I don't want to," Margalo said to Mikey's back as they crossed the long room.

"I know, but you have to. To help me."

"Why can't I help baby-sit instead, and you could split the money with me?"

"Are you kidding? I've got to get something out of all this, if I'm going to be so perfect. What do you think I am, the Baby-sitters Club?"

They were trotting up the staircase, barely listening to one another.

"You think you're cute enough for Baby-sitters Club? If you do, you're dreaming."

They were outside in the sunlight by then, and Mikey shouldered Margalo, because she couldn't think of any other winning response. Margalo danced out of shoulder range and kept on teasing. "This is the thanks I get?"

"For what?"

"For trying to help you."

"Why should I thank you?" Mikey asked. "You

don't want them to get divorced any more than I do."

And that was only the truth, Margalo knew. She started to feel like a balloon somebody was letting the air out of. Why *should* she get thanked when she was just trying to get what she wanted, getting Mikey to stay in Newtown, keeping her own life the way she wanted it.

"But I do thank you," Mikey said, back in control of the conversation.

"For what?"

"For not putting the most obvious thing on that list."

Recess was only half over, so they weren't in any big hurry. Voices floated all around them, and Margalo tried to think of what was the obvious thing she hadn't put on the list. "I don't — " she started to say, and then she did. "You mean go on a diet? But there's no reason for you to do that. You're in great shape."

"Oh, yeah. Alicia Silverstone's dying of jealousy."

"You know what I mean. Honestly, Mikey, you're as bad as your mother. And it's your mother who wants to look like Sharon Stone. That's her problem. Don't you think that's true? She just tries to make it your problem so she won't fail at it. The same way she wants her marriage to be like some TV marriage."

"She knows better than that," Mikey said.

"Does she? Then what's her complaint?"

"I don't know," Mikey told Margalo. "She doesn't confide in me. She just tells me what to do, and what to think, and what's wrong that's keeping me from being as perfect as she wants me to be."

"But Mikey," Margalo said. "Nobody can be perfect, no matter how hard you try."

"I don't see why not," Mikey argued.

"It's impossible, that's why."

"Who says? And so what?"

Sometimes Mikey could drive a person crazy.

"You don't even *want* to be her kind of perfect," Margalo argued.

"I don't want to move, either," Mikey argued. "I'm just trying to take some of the stress out of their lives."

Margalo gave up. You couldn't discuss something with Mikey. It was a waste of energy to even try.

Besides, what if Mikey was right, and she *could* get perfect? Margalo wouldn't put anything past Mikey.

"Tell me how it goes, you will, won't you?" she asked.

6.

Michelle Angela

It was mostly by phone that Margalo heard about the War on Divorce. Mikey didn't talk much about it at school. At school, she cared so little about the divorce that she didn't even notice when people made remarks, not even when Louis Caselli said, "If I were your parents, I'd get divorced too. Just to get away from you." It was Margalo who noticed, and cared; so she spent a few happy days following Louis around at recess, smiling at him whenever he looked at her, trying to get him to talk to her about anything, soccer, what he did in the summer, and if there were some girls he liked more than others, and what bands he listened to. She would call him up at home, too, but never say her name, and ask him personal questions, like what was his favorite breakfast cereal. After about three days of this, everybody knew Margalo Epps had a major crush on Louis Caselli.

Which made Louis miserable. He was embarrassed, and ashamed, and humiliated, because one of the geekiest girls in the sixth grade had a crush on him. "You have to feel sorry for her," he said to his friends, but that didn't stop the teasing.

Margalo snuck into the other sixth-grade classroom and wrote his name on the blackboard — LOUIS FRANCIS PAUL CASELLI — in red chalk. She drew a big red heart around his name, and then outlined that in thick white chalk, then made a scalloped edge of red.

Louis never figured it out.

It took Mikey about one hour to figure it out, and Tanisha only about a day. They told Linny, who told Gianette, and pretty soon all the girls knew. They all watched Margalo act crazy about Louis, and watched Louis trying to get away from her. He'd turn around sometimes and she'd have snuck up behind him, silent, and he'd see her gooey-eyed face, having a crush on him. It made him jump, and it made his friends tease him until his face turned red with impotent fury, which suited Margalo just fine. That would teach him to make jokes about Mikey's divorce.

Mikey might not notice what people said at school, but home was a different matter. Margalo heard two or three times a day on the phone how the Save This Marriage campaign was going. She even helped create Michelle Angela, Perfect Daughter, a job that started with cheerleading Mikey through the cleaning up of her bedroom.

"I can't do it," Mikey's voice wailed down the long thin telephone wires between their houses. "I just can't."

"Yes you can. One step at a time, like they say in rehab. Just Say No to mess. It's simple. First you put all your books in the bookcase — you can do that. Then the papers — go through and throw out what you can, put the rest in a pile in a desk drawer. Do that, and then call me back," Margalo said in a soothing, motherly voice.

"How big a jerk do you think I am?" Mikey demanded.

"About cleaning your room? Do you really want to know?"

Mikey hung up, but later she called back. "Should I tell them?"

"I'd let her find out on her own. She'll like it better if she discovers it herself. If you tell her, she'll just feel like she has to be grateful, or think you think she *ought* to be grateful."

"Then she'll start finding things I didn't do. You're right. I'll just, maybe, leave the door open."

"Or what if you tell her you don't want her nosing around in your room?" Margalo suggested.

"But that's not true. I *do* want her in there."

"That's what I mean," Margalo said.

"Oh," Mikey said. "Wow," she said. "Don't ever go after me, Margalo, Okay?" she said.

"I make no promises," Margalo said, flattered.

"Or maybe you should. I wonder how I'd do if you did."

Margalo could hear Mikey's *Bet-I-Can-Win* smile.

"I bet you couldn't get me," Mikey said.

"I don't have any money to bet with."

"I'll loan you some."

Later Mikey reported the results. "She's all excited. She says, she knew I couldn't avoid growing up forever. She means, turning into a real girl. She's made an appointment for me with her hairdresser. Heidi. Mom wants to know if it's a boy."

"She thinks you're pregnant?" Margalo asked.

Mikey laughed. "She thinks I'm in love. She wants me to be in love. She's ready to give me good advice. It would be a while, I bet, before she starts in on worrying about whether I might get pregnant. First she'll worry about if he'll reject me, or get away from me. Should I pretend that she's right? She'd like that. It's what girls my age are supposed to do, fall in love with some jerk."

"How about Louis?" That would add to Louis's misery, always a good idea.

"You're already doing Louis. Can't I have somebody a person might like, like Ira? It's not as if he'd ever look at me. He'd even look at *you* before me."

This, Margalo thought, was probably Mikey's idea of a compliment.

"Or Harvey. No, listen, Harvey's perfect, he's African-American, she'd have a fit. She'd have three fits."

"I thought you were trying to be the perfect daughter."

"Okay. So I'll tell her I'm not in love. But I'm not going to tell her the truth."

"Why not? If she knows how much you want her to be pleased with you, won't she pay more attention to what you want? Most people, if they think you care about them, they care about you."

"Not her. The way Mom works, when she's got power she uses it. I'm safer if she thinks I don't care. Dad never learned that. Poor guy," Mikey said. "Do you think my father's a wimp?"

Margalo stuck to the point. "Are you going to go to this Heidi hairdresser?"

"You have to come too. We're going to the mall, Saturday," Mikey answered. "You said you would. All day. She says I'm an all-day job. But she's teaching me how to make a meat loaf tonight."

Margalo didn't mind a day at the mall, except that Mrs. Elsinger drove them there, and part of the trip took place on an expressway. Except for the drive, Margalo was sort of looking forward to the day.

The mall had been built just beyond the city limits. It looked like a spaceship, with parking pods all around it. It was modern enough to have a couple of fountain areas, and large enough to be anchored at one end by a Sears and the other by a MacLeod's, although it wasn't one of the newest, largest malls, the kind with two stories and glass elevators. Mikey and Margalo followed Mrs. Elsinger from the car to the entrance. "No wonder you don't like going to the mall," Margalo said. "My pulse probably hit 250 when she passed that Lexus."

"I don't know what your problem is. I have to ride in the suicide seat," Mikey answered.

"Don't dawdle." Mrs. Elsinger was holding the heavy glass door open for them. "You aren't getting cold feet, are you?"

"You get an airbag," Margalo pointed out to Mikey.

"We aren't looking for airbags," Mrs. Elsinger said. "Half the time I don't know what you two are talking about." Mrs. Elsinger wore low-heeled shoes, for a day's shopping, and loose trousers. She had a list in her purse. Mikey and Margalo wore jeans and sneakers, but nicer-than-usual tops. "Shall we start in lingerie?" Mrs. Elsinger asked, leading them into the perfumed, musicked, muffled air of the department store. She led them through men's shoes, and shirts, past women's daytime wear — lingering briefly to admire a cream-colored gabardine pantsuit on a manikin whose head and hands had been amputated — toward racks of nightgowns and slips, and walls of bras and underpants.

"What do you think?" Mrs. Elsinger was already excited by what a good time they were having. "Some of those cute panties, and I think you're ready for training bras." A saleswoman, as dressed up as Mrs. Elsinger, approached them and Mrs. Elsinger greeted her. "Can you fit my daughter with a training bra?"

Mikey didn't even protest. Mikey just let herself be led away by her mother; but Margalo wasn't about to go with them, and they didn't ask her.

Margalo had time to cruise the section three times, examining nightgowns and robes, as well as negligees that were, as far as she could tell, bathrobes that cost more and covered less, figuring out how much she could spend — if she didn't care how much she spent — on a pair of underpants. She thought about those words, *negligee, lingerie, brassiere* — fancy, floppy French words. Two saleswomen had come up to her, either to see if they could help her, or to catch her shoplifting. Finally the Elsingers reappeared. "What did you get?" Margalo asked Mikey. She knew she was supposed to be interested, and maybe a little jealous; she knew the role she was there to play.

"Show her, Mikey," Mrs. Elsinger urged.

Mikey picked underpants up one by one from the mound on the counter.

"Neat," Margalo said, the right thing. "Cool."

Mikey named the colors, and she actually

didn't sound sarcastic. "Blue Moon. Pumpkin Pie. Roses Are Red. Lemonade. Key Lime. Purple Passion."

"Neat," Margalo said, right and right again. "Cute."

"I'll be paying by check," Mrs. Elsinger told the saleslady. Mrs. Elsinger always paid by check, when she could, or cash. She worked for a bank, and so she knew who really profited from credit cards. "Don't think that banks are run to benefit the customers," she often told Mikey and Margalo. Paying by check took a little longer, but according to Mrs. Elsinger it was worth the trouble. The saleslady started ringing in their purchases. Mrs. Elsinger kept an eye on her.

"So," Mikey said.

"So," Margalo said.

"I do kind of like the colors," Mikey admitted.

"Me too. They're great."

"I tried on a bra. She brought three in, but she didn't stay."

"Good," Margalo said.

"Training bras. Training for what? That's what I want to know."

"I want to know what's being trained," Margalo said.

They backed away from the counter, not to be overheard.

"Like some bridle for a horse you're breaking in," Mikey said.

"Weird," Margalo agreed. "Aurora doesn't wear bras."

"Even when she exercises?"

"Aurora doesn't exercise. She hates bras."

"Maybe," Mikey suggested, "there are some breasts you just can't train."

"If there are, I hope I inherit them from her."

"And who's the trainer, I want to know that, too," Mikey said. "So what did you do?"

"Lurked. Tried to get arrested for shoplifting."

"You didn't succeed," Mikey observed.

"No," Margalo agreed.

"Maybe next time," Mikey said.

Their next stop was Junior Girls, where Mikey tried on whatever her mother liked. Some of them her mother liked enough to buy. All Mikey said about any of them was "Fine by me."

Margalo couldn't understand why Mrs. Elsinger didn't see right through Mikey.

Next Mrs. Elsinger tried on the cream-colored pantsuit. "It's my turn," she said, and they didn't argue. They waited in a pair of chairs for her to come out and show them how good she looked.

Margalo looked at Mikey, sitting with a pile of shopping bags at her feet.

Mikey looked at Margalo. "I can't believe we're here. Doing this."

"Anyway, she's having a good time."

"What am I going to do with all these things she's buying?"

Mrs. Elsinger needed shoes for her new suit, a couple of blouses, and then she sent the girls out to the car to put their shopping bags into the trunk. "I'll meet you by the fountain," she told Mikey, giving her the car keys. "We just have time for lunch before your hair appointment."

"We won't be long," Mikey assured her mother.

It was almost not like being with Mikey at all. "Is this how you're acting all the time?" Margalo asked. She was impressed.

Mikey nodded grimly.

"Is it working?"

Mikey shrugged, grimly.

"How long can you do it for?"

"As long as it takes," Mikey announced grimly. "But can I come to your house for the night tonight?"

After lunch, during which everybody let Mrs. Elsinger order chef's salads for them all, they came out of the restaurant, and a little dark-haired, dark-eyed girl came dancing up to them. "Everybody is here!" she announced. It was Gianette, of course, and "Oh, you are with your mother," she said to Margalo, getting it wrong, of course, then, "Oh, you are Mikey's mother. But Mikey, you have a chance to turn out pretty, with such a pretty mother," she said, and then, "We are all here for the whole afternoon. I am Gianette St. Etienne," she introduced herself to Mrs. Elsinger.

"You aren't from around here," Mrs. Elsinger said.

"I have moved from New Or-le-ans," Gianette answered. "It is very different here."

"New Orleans is pretty different from any-where else," Mrs. Elsinger said.

"Except, they say, in Europe. They say Paris," Gianette said. She chatted quite happily with Mikey's mother. She wore another twirly skirt, in a red bandanna fabric, and big gold hoops in her ears. "Maybe I will go to Paris, someday."

"Well," Mrs. Elsinger said. "Maybe you will." Gianette stayed there, smiling at Mikey's mother, as if she was expecting to be invited along. "We have a hair appointment," Mrs. Elsinger said.

"I am pleased to meet you," Gianette said, sadly.

As they walked away, Mrs. Elsinger remarked, "That's a pretty child, interesting, a little forlorn. She must be one of your new friends," Mrs. Elsinger decided.

Outside the entrance to Snippers, a man stopped right in front of them. "Patty? This is a surprise," he said. He was tall and tanned and muscular, in his polo shirt, blue-eyed and self-satisfied, a cheerful kind of man, full of jokes about roses between two thorns, just kidding kids, full of information about a sale in sports clothing, including shoes, his face full of smiles, as if meeting up with Mrs. Elsinger made his day. Mrs. Elsinger was cheerful right back at him, saying, "Poor Mikey got the Wicked Witch of the West for a mother." Mikey said, "You're not wicked," and Mrs. Elsinger just laughed, as did her friend. Gary. "You know what I mean," Mrs. Elsinger said, and "It's okay," Mikey said. "We're having a girls' day out," Mrs. Elsinger said to Gary.

"Can you interrupt it to come look at the sale with me? I'd like your advice on a pair of shorts," Gary asked. Mrs. Elsinger hesitated; then she sent Mikey and Margalo into Snippers. "You sign in and then you always have to wait, anyway, and there's no reason we all have to wait, is there?"

Margalo wondered, but did not ask, if Gary was

the boyfriend Mrs. Elsinger denied having. She'd never seen Mikey's mother as cheerful as she was when she walked off with him.

When Mrs. Elsinger joined them on the waiting-area couch, Mikey asked, "Are all the guys at your health club so — healthy?"

Mrs. Elsinger laughed. "You mean handsome."

"I didn't say it," Mikey said.

"Gary's one of our better specimens. Did you like him?"

How could either one of them have any opinion of someone they'd only seen for a couple of minutes, being jovial at them? Margalo thought. No matter how handsome he was. But, "He seemed nice," Mikey said, and Mrs. Elsinger seemed pleased to hear that.

When they were finally called, they were ushered back behind a low glass wall, which shielded them from anyone passing down the mall walkways, to a young woman who waited for them beside the kind of chair haircutters and dentists have. She wore a white medical coat and had a towel in her hands. Her hair was perfect, every wave curved just right, and no matter how she moved, her hair stayed still. Mrs. Elsinger announced, "Here we are, at long last. Heidi, this is Mikey. What do you think?" she asked Heidi. "Suddenly she wants to be a real girl. We think it's love, don't we, Margalo?"

Margalo thought she would choke to death, and when she looked at Mikey in the mirror, she thought Mikey already had. What planet was Mrs. Elsinger living on? You couldn't be an investment banker and still be stupid, could you?

When Mikey had had her hair washed by Heidi, and wrapped in a short pink towel that matched the narrow pink towel wrapped around Mikey's neck, which matched the pink plastic sheet draped over her body, so that she sat in the elevated chair like some head-only monster in a *Star Wars* movie, Mrs. Elsinger started deciding what new style Heidi should choose for Mikey. "Short, layered back at the side, soft bangs," Mrs. Elsinger said. "Don't you agree? Shaped at the back of her head. Those half bangs, feathery. Something pretty."

Mikey made faces at Margalo in the mirror. "Mom?" she started to say.

Mrs. Elsinger interrupted. "I hope you're having a good time, Mikey. I certainly am."

Margalo guessed Mrs. Elsinger might have been a better mother with another kind of daughter than Mikey was. But that didn't help Mikey. Margalo had seen Mikey looking terrible like this before —

like last year when nobody voted for her for class president. Margalo could guess how badly Mikey wanted this to be all over, so she could go home and be herself.

Except Mikey would go home and keep on trying to be Mrs. Elsinger's dream daughter. It was time for Margalo to step in.

"If you wear your hair short like that," Margalo said to Mikey's face in the mirror, "it'll be neat. Just like Ronnie and Linny, and Anneliese, and Sharon, LJ, Karen. Lindsay, too, she's just had hers cut short." She explained to Mrs. Elsinger, "It's sort of like, all the girls in the sixth grade belong together. Except me, because Aurora cuts my hair and she's not a professional, she can only cut it straight, and Rhonda, who has long blond hair, and the African-American girls, of course. But they're different."

"Everybody is wearing short hair at school?" Mrs. Elsinger asked. "Mikey never tells me anything about styles. But that little Gianette wasn't."

"Hers is too curly," Margalo said. "Gianette has her own style, she looks like a Gypsy, don't you think? She's unusual looking, isn't she?" Well, that was true. It wasn't as if Margalo was saying anything positive about Gianette.

"*All* the other girls?" Mrs. Elsinger mused.

"It's the look, this year," Heidi chimed in. "Two years ago they all wanted a flip."

"Mikey will fit right in, it'll be great," Margalo said.

Mrs. Elsinger wasn't pleased by this. "Mikey? Is that what you want? Just because you're in love? To fit right in?"

"Not particularly," Mikey answered.

"Then why are you insisting on having your hair styled the way everyone else has?" Mrs. Elsinger asked. "I wish you'd listen to me, just this once, and let it grow. It was lovely when you had long hair. Why not just ask Heidi for a trim, to even it and for the split ends, maybe a little shaping. Could you show her how to comb in just the slightest wave, Heidi?"

"Simple is always in style, classic," Heidi agreed.

Margalo crossed her eyes at Mikey in the mirror, so quick it was as good as invisible.

When they were finished at the mall, it turned out that Mikey couldn't spend the night at Margalo's because her mother had promised her baby-sitting services to a friend at work, who was a single parent and this was her first date in six months. "A blind date, so it won't last long," Mikey told Margalo, "so I won't have to baby-sit for long, but I still can't sleep over."

"Just because he's blind doesn't mean she won't have a good time," Margalo said.

"You know what we mean," Mrs. Elsinger said, half-looking over her shoulder at Margalo, half-watching the road as the Audi zipped across two lanes of traffic to make a quick left turn.

"I made twelve dollars," Mikey told Margalo on the phone the next morning. "Plus a tip. A two-dollar tip. She had three kids, we played Monopoly, and I creamed them. That's fourteen dollars."

"Can't you get me a baby-sitting job too?" Margalo asked.

"Don't you want me to earn money? My allowance isn't very big."

"I don't even have an allowance," Margalo pointed out.

"Too bad for you," Mikey said.

Margalo reminded herself that whenever they went out and spent money, it was Mikey's money they spent.

"Maybe your mother has other friends I could work for?" she asked.

"Probably. She thinks you're perfect, anyway, just because you're skinny."

Margalo reminded herself that Mikey was worried about her parents getting a divorce.

"Dad gave me a lesson," Mikey said.

"Tennis?"

"This morning. And I wasn't bad. He says I have a natural aptitude."

"You're a good athlete," Margalo reminded her.

"You'll have to learn tennis too."

"I don't have a racquet."

"We have old ones. My mom used to play too."

"I don't like sports."

"You can learn."

"I don't want to," Margalo said.

"That doesn't matter."

"Oh. Ah. Well," Margalo said, getting more and more sarcastic until Mikey finally got it. "In *that* case."

"What if it turns out you *are* good at it?" Mikey demanded. "What if you like it? You might. You could. He wants to take me to the movies next weekend and have supper at McDonald's, and he wants you to come too. It's the new Disney."

"I hate Disney movies," Margalo protested.

"I know."

"And so do you."

"I know, but he wants to. He hates them too," Mikey said. "But he wants to be a father taking his daughter to a Disney movie, because that's what fathers do. And daughters."

"He says, would we rather play miniature golf?" Mikey said later in the week.

"Much rather," Margalo said.

"And you try to tell me you're not athletic," Mikey said.

Margalo didn't bother responding to something that stupid.

"You *know* I think miniature golf is boring," Mikey reminded her.

If they'd been in the same room and not talking on the phone, Margalo would have crossed her eyes at Mikey. Instead she put a cross-eyed question to Mikey. "If you had to choose between having Pocahantas's hair and Simba's uncle, which would you take?"

Mikey took a while over that one. "The uncle. He has better songs."

"Well then."

"Miniature golf is shorter than a movie."

"So we'll do that?"

"And it's outside. Sort of outside, anyway. Except for being next to the highway, and all the lights, and the people, and the smell of fried food."

"You're not trying to have a good time," Margalo reminded Mikey. "You're just trying to be perfect."

"I hope they appreciate all the trouble I'm going to," Mikey said.

They didn't. Margalo didn't say that, but she thought it, and she thought Mikey thought the same.

Eating supper at McDonald's, where Mr. Elsinger ordered the Arch Deluxe burger as well as a Big Mac, "to make a true comparison," then going across the street to the miniature golf course and then, after three rounds of that, returning to McDonald's, for soft ice cream, or sodas, or McNuggets — it was weird, from beginning to end, entirely a weird evening.

There were many weird things, like the way Mr. Elsinger kept saying that they couldn't do this if Patty were with them, could they? Or the way their little group swung like a pendulum, between the restaurant and the golf course. Or especially the way all night long, Mikey kept talking to her father about work.

They sat with food juices dribbling down onto their trays, and Mikey explained to her father,

"You're a man. That means you have to work all of your life. Mostly."

"Unless I strike it rich," he agreed. "Win the lottery. Win the Publishers Clearinghouse sweepstakes. Invent a better mousetrap or a better Microsoft, write a bestseller."

"Rob a bank," Mikey suggested.

"Rob a bank and get away with it," he said.

"So what makes your job a good one?" Mikey asked.

"Nothing," Mr. Elsinger joked. Margalo was watching this. Mr. Elsinger pulled his mouth back into a smile shape that had no smiling in it, and no anger, either. "But at least," Mr. Elsinger said, "I don't have to do back-breaking physical labor from sunup to sundown, the way the serfs did in the Middle Ages. I think it's important to look on the bright side, don't you?"

Margalo nodded.

Mikey disagreed. "I think it's important to move over to the bright side," she said.

"There's a lot of your mother in you," her father said.

"If you don't like it, why don't you change jobs?"

"Who said I didn't like it?" he asked. "I don't, as it happens. But you didn't hear me say that, did you? I'm not a complainer," he told them. "You'll find this out soon enough — most people don't enjoy their jobs."

"How'd you like the Arch burger?" Margalo asked Mr. Elsinger.

He thought about the question. "It's slippy," he answered. "They must think adults can handle the tomato and lettuce slipping one way, the hamburger another. Do you want to get one, and try? It could be a test of how mature you are. Would you two girls like to take a maturity test?"

As they crossed over to the golf course, Mikey raised the question of work again. Margalo had never heard Mr. Elsinger talk so much. He told them about health and retirement benefits, the differences between long- and short-range objectives; he explained marketing strategies and considered what you needed to understand in order to work well in an office. "Women aren't just secretaries these days," he told Mikey, and Margalo, too.

They knew that, they told him.

"You're going to have to work all your lives too, probably," he told them. "So you should understand that it's not a bed of roses out there. In the workplace. Ask your mother."

"She likes her job," Mikey argued.

"I know. It makes me jealous."

"Why don't you find a job you like?" Mikey asked. "I thought programmers could always find work. Isn't someone writing interesting programs? Or you could start a company with some other people, the way you did in the city."

"That was about perfect. Wasn't it?" Mr. Elsinger asked, with another lifeless smile.

Margalo could almost read Mikey's mind. It read: Why did I bring up *that* subject?

"I'm trying for a hole in one on the next one," Mikey said. "You want to bet a quarter I make it?"

"I'll bet a quarter you don't," Margalo offered.

"You don't have any money," Mikey pointed out. "What about you, Dad? You want to bet on me? Or against me?"

"We need my salary," Mr. Elsinger explained as they waited in line for their turn. Margalo hammered at the side of her sneakers with the club, pretending she was on television, warming up for the big putt. She thought: She had never been so bored in her life, and she hoped Mikey appreciated it, but she was pretty sure Mikey didn't. Mr. Elsinger talked on, "My point is, my salary helps maintain our standard of living. And I do like the money. It *is* more than I ever made in the city. Besides, I couldn't go back anyway. They've replaced me, long ago, and they're doing just fine without me, and besides, maybe it was only the three of us who just happened to work together well. Probably it wouldn't happen again, with another group," he told them.

Now Margalo was getting depressed.

"But it's a relief to talk about it," Mr. Elsinger said. "I'm feeling a little better about my life tonight. You two are good company."

Mikey telephoned Margalo after her babysittees were all in bed. "I think it's working. I think they're getting along better. Do you think it was me all the time? Do you really think I'm that stressful a person?"

"Can you keep this up for six years?" Margalo asked.

"No," Mikey said. "I'm never having children."

"Me neither. They're expensive," Margalo agreed.

"When you don't like them. I think I'll just run away from home."

"Say, that's a smart idea. That's really smart. That'll solve *everything.*"

"Well, they'd be happier. I'm the only one who wouldn't be. I like having a home, and my own room, my own beds from my grandmother. You wouldn't be happier either, would you? If I ran away?"

It was time for a joke. "That depends," Margalo said.

"What? Depends? Depends on what?" Mikey demanded.

"On if you'll leave me your training bra."

"I'll leave you all of them," Mikey laughed. "I'll even give them to you right away. Tomorrow. In school. I'll bring them to school in a plain brown paper bag, unmarked."

"I want the bag marked," Margalo argued. "TRAINING BRAS, in capitals, with red Magic Marker, so everyone can see."

"They'd be embarrassed, especially the boys, but everyone, too. They'd die of embarrassment," Mikey said. "But *I* wouldn't. And neither would you. Maybe I'll do it. If I do, you have to take them."

"Says who?"

"Mar-galo," Mikey protested. "This is all your idea."

"Says who?"

"Besides, I can't," Mikey said. "I'd probably get detention, and that would ruin everything."

7.

A Therapeutic Failure

"Did you know," Mikey demanded, "they've been going for counseling? Marriage counseling?"

Even over the phone, where she couldn't see Mikey's face, Margalo recognized that smiling, slit-eyed fury. "How would I know?" she demanded right back.

"If she told Aurora."

"Why would she do that? They're not even friends. Aurora doesn't trust her."

"That makes them even, then, because she says

she doesn't trust Aurora to have any standards." Mikey calmed down. "So I guess I really can't come live with you."

Mikey's anger was the gusty-windy sort. It blew up, and blew around, then blew over. Margalo could never predict how long it would last. All she knew for sure was that once it rose up, it would settle back down.

Temporarily.

Margalo went back to the main subject of the phone call. "Do they like the counseling?"

Wrong question.

"They never even told me," Mikey said, gusting angry again. "Of course he wouldn't, he's never said a word about the divorce, not a peep out of him on that subject. But you'd think she'd tell me. Two months, they've been going for two months."

"But Mikey, it was only less than a month ago that she told *you*. It wasn't even a month ago."

"Tell me about it."

Margalo thought she knew what was going on with the Elsingers. But she didn't know if now was a good time to tell Mikey what she thought.

"So what do you think?" Mikey asked. "What should I do? To keep them from doing it, getting divorced."

Margalo took a breath.

"Well?" Mikey asked.

Sometimes you just had to tell people the truth.

"Answer me," Mikey demanded.

"I don't think there's anything you *can* do," Margalo said.

"You're a big help," Mikey said, and hung up.

"They want me to go," Mikey said.

Margalo clutched the phone. "Where?" she asked. Even as close as the city wouldn't be close enough, once someone moved away from being in the same school.

"To marriage counseling."

"Oh." Margalo's whole torso relaxed.

"I'm not even married," Mikey protested. "He wants me to."

"Your father?"

"The counselor."

"It's a man?"

"She prefers working with men. Dr. Taylor. He's the one who asked me to come too, so he can get an idea of the family dynamics. Did Aurora ever do that to you?"

"No, but — "

Mikey waited about half a second, then demanded, "But what?"

"The thing is, he was in love, but not with her. I mean, he never was in love with her, but it was different when he was in love with somebody else."

"Stick to the point, Margalo. If you didn't want the divorce, what did you do about it?"

"I'm not like you, Mikey. I don't *do* things to get my own way."

Mikey didn't say a word.

Well, Margalo could see why. She asked, "Are you going to go see this counselor?"

"Do you think if he thinks I'm psychologically damaged — what do they say, 'at risk'? If he thinks I'm at risk, would he tell them to stay together or tell them to split up?" Mikey asked.

Margalo raised other possibilities. "Maybe he'd have you locked up in a loony bin. Or put into foster care?"

"I don't think I'd enjoy a loony bin."

"I'd bake you a cake with a file in it. Or cookies, with a lot of little files, one in each. I'd cut up emery boards."

"Did I tell you? I made lasagna sauce last night. And it was good, too. And it's not at all hard to make. I don't know why she complains so much. About having to cook."

"She likes to cook," Margalo pointed out.

"So it's the having-to that she doesn't like? Do you think I'm just like my mother? No, don't answer that." And Mikey hung up.

"I don't have to go if I don't want to," Mikey said. "I don't want to."

Margalo tried to prepare herself for bad news before she asked, "Go where?"

"To the marriage doctor. The doctor who cures sick marriages. Margalo, did Aurora cry?"

"Aurora cries a lot. You know that."

"I don't mean now, I mean when she and what's-his-face were getting divorced, when he was in love with somebody else."

"Oh. Then. Yes, a lot. Really a lot. Sometimes it lasted all day long. We'd leave for school in the morning — you know, damp sandwiches?"

"I'm serious," Mikey announced.

"I almost am," Margalo said. "And she'd still be drizzling away when we got home. He wouldn't come home for dinner. Well, I almost didn't blame him. She'd just be — weeping at him, into his noodles. I did blame him, of course, but — Is your mother crying?" she asked.

"You're kidding," Mikey said.

"So she isn't."

"Mom doesn't cry, you know that. Crying's weak. Mom's strong. Crying's for sissies, and you don't think my mom's a sissy, do you? No, it's my dad. He sometimes — cries — not much, but — when they get back from seeing Dr. Taylor. Sometimes. So I can't see why I should go. And sometimes Dad gets weepy — you know, sniffles? — when they've been talking about, like, who'll get the turkey platter some friends gave them for a wedding present. Or the desk, because it's an antique. They bought it together. The cars are no problem, because they each have their own."

"I thought Dr. Taylor was a marriage counselor."

"He is."

"I thought, that means they're talking about staying married."

"As opposed to divvying up the loot?" Mikey asked. "You'd think, wouldn't you? So what could I say to him anyway? Except they shouldn't be doing this to me."

"Does Dr. Taylor know you're against the divorce?"

"I don't know."

"He might want to know what your reaction is."

"I'm not even sure he knows they have a child."

"He has to, Mikey, if he says he wants to talk to you."

"But do I want to talk to him? That's the question. Unless there's something *he* could do to stop them."

"They keep trying to talk to me about it. Why do they keep trying to talk to me? They don't have anything new to tell me."

"Maybe you should come to my house for the weekend," Margalo suggested. "Maybe you need a break."

"I can't. I don't know what they'd do if I wasn't here to stop them, go out and get some quickie divorce, fly to Mexico or something. I don't dare leave them alone for long. But the Tiltons are going out both nights this weekend, so I'll be baby-sitting. Maybe I could live with the Tiltons and be their maid."

"You'd make a terrible maid."

"The kids love my chocolate-chip cookies," Mikey said.

"I thought you didn't like baby-sitting. I thought, you were just doing this to make your mother happy. Is she?"

"I guess. I mean, she hasn't told me the things I'm doing wrong when I baby-sit, so I guess Mr. Tilton hasn't been complaining about me at work. And I haven't broken any of the children. Yet."

"I wish I had a baby-sitting job."

"No you don't. It's lucky for me that I know Aurora or I'd never have any idea how it's supposed to be done. They never leave you alone, until they go to bed, and they never want to go to bed."

"You don't have to do it."

"I like earning money. Earning money is better than being given an allowance, you know?"

"No. I don't," Margalo pointed out.

"Then go out and get a job," Mikey advised unsympathetically.

Margalo believed in fighting fire with fire, an eye with an eye. "So are you giving up your allowance?"

"Are you kidding me?" Mikey demanded.

"What are you going to do with all the money you're saving?" Margalo asked. "I wish you'd ask your mother to find me a baby-sitting job too."

"Ask her yourself. She likes you better anyway."

That might be true, Margalo realized. Although, she thought, it probably wasn't. Wasn't blood thicker than water?

Although, Howie and Esther chose to stay with Aurora, so maybe being a good mother was thicker than water.

Although, Mrs. Elsinger wasn't much of a mother, so if she preferred Margalo to Mikey, did that mean Margalo wasn't much of a daughter? If she was the kind of daughter a kind of mother like Mikey's would prefer to have?

And what did any of that matter, if she could find Margalo a baby-sitting job and Margalo could earn some money?

"Maybe I will," Margalo said.

"I think you ought to. Then, if I have to run away, I'll have whatever you've saved up as well as whatever I have."

"Running away is stupid," Margalo reminded Mikey.

"Not if you're smart about it," Mikey answered.

"And you'd be smart?"

"I'm smart enough to know I don't want to have to run away," Mikey pointed out. "This conversation is what's stupid," she said. "You can tell

I'm not adopted, because I'm just as stupid as they are," she said. And hung up.

Once everyone already knew about it, Mikey would sometimes start in talking about her parents' divorce at school, over lunch in the cafeteria, where she had an audience already in their seats. It turned out Mikey could be funny, like when she made fun of her father for getting weepy over TV ads where somebody called home to tell her father how much she appreciated him. "I mean, the TV screen is filling up with sweetness," Mikey said, "like fake maple syrup from the supermarket, fake, cheap maple syrup that makes your teeth ache it's so sweet. And there he is, sitting there, sniveling into his Kleenex. He's going nuts. He's cracking up. And he doesn't even love her."

"How do you know that?"

"And meanwhile she's going around the house with her yellow legal pad, making lists of everything, and how much it cost, and how much she wants it. In columns. Her grandmother's hairbrush. His grandmother's mirror."

A lot of people tried to be sympathetic to Mikey, to be understanding and particularly nice, but when she wasn't nicer back, things pretty quickly returned to normal. So when Mikey said her parents were aliens from another planet, somebody — usually Ronnie or Tanisha — would say, "Now we know why you're so weird." And Margalo would help Mikey out, asking, "What about the omelette pan? Has that been settled yet? They're having big fights over who gets the omelette pan," she told Mikey's audience.

Even though neither of the Elsingers ate eggs anymore. Mikey's father was watching his cholesterol and Mikey's mother was eating low fat.

Somewhere in there, from the other end of the long table, Gianette would start in on one of her endless creepy stories about some love spell the *belle-dame* had cast, or some voodoo doll she was sticking pins in, or about the ghosts in the ruined mansion to which her house was the gate house. Mikey would just cut Gianette off. "She hid the omelette pan in with her sweaters. It took him days to find it. He moved it to the box of weights she gave him for his fortieth birthday, out in the garage. She's still looking."

"I spect your family is dysfunctional," Gianette would say. "Tell us, is anybody happy to be in your family, Mikey?"

"The cat," Mikey said, with a smile that

wouldn't have fooled anyone. "The cat is pretty content."

Gianette dismissed that. "Cats are always content, as long as they are fed. The cat doesn't count," she proclaimed, and didn't realize until everyone laughed that Mikey was making fun of her.

Then they were finished with lunch. Mikey piled up trays, Margalo's on top of hers, Ronnie's making the third. When Mikey piled up trays, she didn't bother to move the bowls and plates and milk cartons; she just made a rackety, tippy, messy stack of trays. Instead of carrying the stack back to the dish counter, she smashed them down on top of Derrie's tray.

And walked away.

"Mikey?" Derrie called to her back.

Mikey turned around.

"I don't want these."

Mikey headed off.

"Mikey!"

Mikey turned around again.

Derrie said, "You think, just because we feel sorry for you? You think we'll let you do whatever you feel like? And win everything?"

Mikey said, "What's to *win*?" and she turned

on her heels and ran off, leaving Derrie with the pile of dirty trays. Derrie sighed and picked up the pile. "That's not very nice," she complained.

A milk carton tottered onto the floor. Two spoons clattered after it.

Everyone watched Derrie and hoped. If the stack tumbled onto the floor, it would make a pretty big noise. It would make a pretty big mess, too, and nobody wanted to miss that, if it happened. Derrie was like a circus performer, in the center ring with the spotlight on her.

When Mikey came back carrying another tray and plopped it right on top of the four Derrie was balancing, everyone laughed, even Derrie.

Laughing, of course, made the trays wobble, and teeter.

By the time Miss Brinson got there from the back of the cafeteria, it was too late for anything but cleaning up.

"I'm going," Mikey announced to Margalo, on the phone.

Margalo didn't want to ask, but she did. "Going where?"

"To marriage counseling. If I ever get married, it'll give me practice."

"What will you tell the counselor?"

"Dr. Taylor? It depends on what he asks me."

"Whose side will you be on?"

"Mine," Mikey answered. "Whose do you think?"

"He doesn't look like a therapist," Mikey reported. "He looks like some tennis player. No wonder my mother likes him. He's got short hair — blond — and he wears a tweed jacket. He sits behind his desk and I sat between them, in chairs. As if he was a principal and I was in trouble. But they're the ones. It's not fair."

"You never mind being in trouble," Margalo pointed out.

"When it's not my fault I do."

"So what did he say?"

"He wanted — get this — he wanted everyone to say three good things about everybody else. Both of them first, then me."

"And did they?"

"She said he was unaggressive — big compliment from her, right? She said he genuinely wants to do things right and that was something. Then she said he hadn't done drugs at all since we moved here."

"Is that true? It's been over a year. Does that mean he's cured?"

"Well, listen to this. It was — weird, it was — Dr. Taylor asked me what I knew about my dad and drugs, so I told him."

"What did you tell him?"

"The truth. That I knew about it, and I remembered being frightened by him. Dr. Taylor said, 'Tell her, Anders.' Dad told me he'd done some drugs, and he remembered the times he scared me, and he wished he hadn't. He said he could promise me it would never happen again. But he was really sorry about it. Then he looked at my mother. Hard."

"Why?"

"And she said to him, 'I had to tell her. Didn't I?' she asked Dr. Taylor, and reminded him that he told them all along that things are better out in the open. So what was so wrong with telling me? Talking it over with me, about his addiction. And Dr. Taylor looked at my father — like some kind of referee — until my father said, 'It wasn't addiction, Patty. That wasn't fair.' And my mother said, 'I was thinking about what was best for Mikey.' "

And her nose shot out across the room, Margalo thought, like Pinocchio's. She didn't say that, though. Instead she said, "Hunnh," to show she was listening.

"Maybe Dr. Taylor's right about having things out in the open, though. I feel better, now I know what exactly happened."

"After that, what did he say was good about her?"

"He said she was successful, and didn't let anything slide, and worked hard."

"Uh-oh," Margalo said.

"Tell me about it," Mikey said. "Maybe they used up the really good things before I got there."

"What about you?"

"I couldn't think up anything good about either one of them. And I didn't want to."

"No, I mean, what did they say about you?"

"Oh. Mom said I could be quite pretty, when I tried, and I seemed to have made a giant step forward in taking responsibility around the house, and I was in love."

Mikey waited.

"But," Margalo said.

Mikey kept on waiting.

"But you're not in love. Are you?"

"Dad said I'm a good athlete, and not vain, and he likes my attitude, I've got spirit."

"That's okay," Margalo said. "That's four," she pointed out.

"And we had to say 'Thank you' each time, after everyone finished. So when Dr. Taylor told me it was my turn, there was this whole long silence, from everyone. Because when therapists hear somebody not answering, they aren't like real people, they don't start talking. He just sat there and waited. Watching me."

"What did you *do*?" Margalo could practically see the scene. She was willing to bet that Mikey stared right back at Dr. Taylor.

"I kept quiet. I looked him in the eye. I figured I could hold out longer than he could. And I was right."

Now Margalo waited, silent, on the phone.

"Finally he said to me, 'You're angry, aren't you?' I thought, For this they're paying you a hundred and twenty-five dollars an hour? I said, 'Of course I'm angry. They're ruining my life.' Dr. Taylor sort of got this little smile on his face. You know? When people think they already know something you're just figuring out?"

Margalo knew, but she'd have thought a therapist would have been too smart to try that with Mikey.

"And he said, 'My guess is you've always been an angry person.' So I let him have it," Mikey's voice said through the receiver. "I told him how sorry they were to have a kid. That got them going, of course. She started in on how young she was when I was born. 'Twenty-eight,' I told her, 'is not young,' and she told me she *felt* young. Too young to have a baby. Then my dad piped in, that he'd had trouble relating to me when I was a baby, and little, but he'd been enjoying being a father once I got older. Dr. Taylor asked him if he had any ideas about what had changed, but my mother horned in to tell us about how much she loved her little baby, how adorable I was, and smarter than any of the other babies. I walked when I was just nine months old, did you know that?"

"Ask me if I care," Margalo requested.

"Neither do I," Mikey said. "How old were you? Just out of curiosity."

"Five," Margalo said.

"Five months? That's impossible. Oh, wait, you mean years, you mean — That was a joke, wasn't it?"

Margalo didn't say anything.

"I told him about you."

"Me? Why? Why would you? What did you say?"

"You'd like to know, wouldn't you?" Mikey asked.

And hung up.

Margalo thought about calling Mikey back, to beg her to tell, or to try to trick her into telling, but then Aurora yelled for her to come downstairs to feed Lily her snack, because it was David's birthday and she had to make the cake. Margalo offered to make the cake, but Aurora said, No, she wanted to. "It's important that the mother makes a cake. Or the father, but it should be a parent," Aurora said.

Margalo filled the spoon with Froot Loops and milk and held it out to Lily. Lily leaned her face forward, to get her mouth around it. "Me feed," she said.

Margalo filled the spoon and handed it to the little girl. "But you're not David's mother."

"I am when he's here," Aurora said.

Lily tried to eat cereal through her forehead. It didn't work.

"If he was at his mother's this week, you'd still make him a birthday cake," Margalo told Aurora.

"Because I'd still be here," Aurora argued.

The logic of it escaped Margalo. But the feelings of it were a relief.

At school somebody had stolen money from Miss Brinson's purse, more than once. She wouldn't say how many times, or how much. All she would tell them was that teachers didn't make enough money to have any to spare for stealing. Clark reported a missing two dollars, from inside a library book overdue since last May, and the book, too, was missing from his cubby. "Right. Like we believe that," people said. Everybody knew how careless Clark was about library books. He'd already lost his borrowing privileges until December. Rhonda had been in charge of collecting the book-club order money, and the envelope was gone, stolen, she said; but several people suggested that she'd just lost it, and they thought she had better make it up out of her own money or get her mother to take care of it. Gianette said someone had taken her bus money, a dollar seventy, and now how would she get home? Miss Carter, the school secretary, reimbursed her out of the principal's miscellaneous fund. There was a meeting of both sixth grades about the stealing.

"It has to stop," the teachers said to their classes.

"Talk to Mikey. Mikey likes to break rules," somebody suggested.

"Talk to Margalo. She's sneaky," Rhonda said, which was true, but it wasn't the kind of thing you announced to teachers.

"If there were someone," Gianette said, "probably it's a boy, don't you think? I don't have much sperience, but isn't a boy more likely to break the law than a girl — well, an ordinary girl? A boy who likes to be the boss, and get attention, I would wonder about drugs," Gianette hinted. "Not in our classroom," she reassured everyone.

"I'm not interested in being a policewoman," Miss Brinson said. "Not at the moment. At the moment, I'm concerned that there shouldn't be any more of this. So I ask you not to bring money to school, except if you must. And to be very careful with your money. I myself am going to stop leaving my purse out."

"Yeah," Joshua Rey said. "Because that's like — like asking someone to steal, like tempting him. It's like giving him permission when you make it so easy."

"Do you really believe that, Joshua?" Miss Brinson asked.

The rest of the meeting was spent talking about making choices, and whether honesty paid better than stealing, and what kinds of things made people want to steal other people's money.

It was Margalo who called Mikey, after soccer practice. "What about this stealing. Did you do it?"

"No," Mikey said. "Why would I? Did you?"

"Because of the divorce," Margalo explained.

"What would stealing money do for the divorce? There are other ways to get in trouble, and they're a lot more fun, too. But Margalo, do you think that getting them both furious at me would keep them from being so angry at one another? Sort of like if there's an alien invasion, all the countries of the world will want to make peace with each other?"

"Anyway, it's not me," Margalo said. She thought she believed Mikey, and she believed Mikey believed *her* — which was good, since she wasn't lying. "Then who did it? You know, maybe you did it and don't remember."

"Yeah, but I've got this baby-sitting money saved up, so I don't need to steal any. Maybe I should use it to get a permanent. My mom would go bananas. She'd feel like a totally successful mom, if I got a permanent with my own money. Don't you think?"

"You'd look stupid," Margalo said. "And I think they cost a fortune. I think Aurora told me that once. You could have a home perm. I could help you."

"Why would I want a permanent?" Mikey demanded. She hung up the phone, but called back right away to report that she and her dad were going out for a third tennis lesson. "I'm having a pretty good time," Mikey said. "Playing tennis."

She hung up again.

"She's really mad," Mikey told Margalo. "I've never seen her this mad. I mean, she's yelling at him."

"When Aurora yells, the next thing that happens is she cries, and then he kisses her and they make up." Margalo couldn't keep hope out of her voice. She was sitting on the floor of the bathroom, her back against the closed door, her feet up on the side of the tub. Outside the high window she could see rain falling steadily.

"Making up isn't in the cards. My mother doesn't make up. She wins or she loses. She doesn't make up, and she doesn't give up." Mikey fell silent. "I don't understand why he wants to stay married to her."

"What got her going?"

"The lawyers. His lawyer doesn't want her to have things her lawyer says she should get."

"What's *wrong* with them?" Margalo demanded.

"Good question," Mikey answered. "But you have to remember, she's always been the money boss. I can see her point. The trouble is, they have to split all of her investments. It's the law. A divorcing couple puts everything they own into one big pile, and figure out how much it's worth, then split it in half so they both get the same."

"That's fair."

"Except she thinks because she invested her own earnings in her own name, she shouldn't have to give him any."

"Maybe," Margalo suggested, "she'd rather stay married than give up half of her investments."

"They're still talking to Dr. Taylor. Is that a good sign?"

"I asked Steven, and he said in his experience marriage counselors most of the time make it easier to get an amicable divorce. So the couples don't end up killing each other."

"Do you think they might?" Mikey sounded hopeful. Then her voice fell again. "So I'd have one dead parent and one in jail, which isn't much of an improvement." Then she added, "My college fund is in there too. In their pile."

"Can they do that?" Margalo asked.

"It's not in a trust or anything. So somebody is going to take the money they told me was for me."

"They still have to send you to college, don't they?"

"I don't care. I just don't — Do you remember what Dr. Taylor asked me, last week, when we went back to see him?"

"How you were doing in school, how you were eating and sleeping, whether you could talk to me about it," Margalo recited.

"All that, but at the end he asked me, in this therapist voice, very mellow, 'What about you, Mikey? What do *you* want?' "

"What did you say?"

" 'I want to make them stop this divorce.' "

"Is that really what you want?"

"Yes, since I can't get what I really want, which is to be eighteen and on my own. I do know when something is impossible, like time travel. Maybe I really want to chain them both up in the cellar, except for when I send them out to work so we still have money coming in — just to keep things the way they are until I'm eighteen. Then they'd never have to see me again."

There were things Mikey would talk about on the phone but nowhere else. Steven and Aurora understood, so the five-minute rule was waived for Mikey. Margalo sometimes spent half an hour on the phone with Mikey, and often more than once in an evening. There was always something going on in the Elsingers' unhappy household.

"Now they both want her car," Mikey reported. "It's a much nicer car. It's got heated seats."

"And a sunroof."

"Lower mileage. Also, she wants the china and glassware, because they were wedding gifts, and wedding gifts are traditionally for the bride."

Margalo sat at the top of the stairs. Susanna was taking one of her endless baths. Mikey waited, then said, "Yes. Well. Can you blame her for trying? The silver is automatically hers. It has her initials on it. They aren't quarreling about the silver."

"It's not fair."

"Tell me about it."

"It's not a bit fair. She's trying to take the whole house."

"She says, she's the woman. The house is her territory. He can have the lawn mower."

"Maybe they're joking?"

"It doesn't sound funny to me."

"But you don't always get jokes."

"My beds too. The ones that they gave me from my grandmother, when she died."

Margalo had a sudden image of Mrs. Elsinger like an octopus-vacuum, sucking everything into her huge round belly. Sofas and lamps, Mikey's beds, books, silver, pots and pans. "What about you? What do you get?"

"Zip. Zilch. Zero. I'm a kid, remember? Maybe I'll run away from home and bring them to their senses."

"Yeah, but Mikey, if you did — it wouldn't be like on a TV show. You're not on a TV show. Besides, it's dangerous. Running away, out there. Alone. Especially a girl. Even you, Mikey."

"Then I'll go to the bad. And they'll have to deal with my problems, and they'll come to their senses and everybody will be reunited. Maybe a threat would be enough. I'll tell them if they don't stop the divorce, I'll go to the bad, and — have sex, get pregnant. You know, the usual stuff parents are afraid girls will do — take up drinking, take up drugs, hang around with sleazy boyfriends — "

"You don't want to do any of that," Margalo pointed out.

"All I want is an effective threat. Maybe I should date an older man, a dirty old man — "

"Mikey!"

"You're right," Mikey agreed. "I'd much rather turn to crime. I bet I'd make a good bank robber. Bonnie and Clyde did it wrong, because they kept wanting to be famous. But I only want the money, and for my parents to know about me, so they'll be afraid that if I'm caught, everybody would think they were bad parents — "

"If what people say will stop them, I can think of some good rumors to start," Margalo interrupted.

Mikey didn't pay any attention to Margalo's offer. "I bet I'd be good at being a criminal," she said.

"I bet you would too," Margalo said loyally.

"And you can help," Mikey offered.

8.

Friday the Thirteenth, Part I

So Mikey gave up on being a perfect daughter. "All that's left I haven't tried is running away," she told Margalo at school. "That'll scare them, and they'll turn to each other. They'll turn to each other, and that'll bring them together, and they won't get divorced."

"That's your plan?" Margalo asked. She didn't look impressed.

"Yeah," Mikey said. Mikey *was* impressed, with her plan and also with herself for thinking it up. It was a pretty Margalo sort of plan, in her opinion.

"That's no plan," Margalo said. "It's an idea."

"It's *my* plan."

"I *know* that," Margalo said. "But where are you going to run away to? How long will you stay? Because you're also planning on coming back, aren't you? And how are you going to eat, and what? Are you camping out? You wouldn't go back to the city, would you? Because that's really dangerous, alone on the streets, unless you're staying with someone, and any of your friends' parents would call your parents. So, what *is* your plan?"

"I have money," Mikey said. "I've saved it. From baby-sitting." She felt stupid. Stupid, and angry.

"A motel? Will they let you into a motel alone, do you think? without a car? Or a hotel? How much money?"

"Enough."

"Are you taking a suitcase? They won't let you stay in a hotel without a suitcase, and if you're a kid alone — especially a girl alone — they'd probably call the police. They *should*. Call the police I mean, because . . . Mikey, some people, if they think you're helpless, that brings out the worst in them. I better come with you," Margalo said.

"I didn't ask you," Mikey said.

Margalo ignored that. "We need to decide where to go, and not until next weekend because I'm going to be at your house for the weekend anyway. Remember? Because Aurora's taking Steven to a wedding all weekend, it's her high-school girlfriend. So they won't be home to worry about me, and the little kids will be at Steven's parents, everybody's going somewhere else. So nobody will call home about me. When the police start looking for us."

"The police?" Mikey hadn't thought of that. That would be exciting, hiding from the police while they searched for her. But Margalo was taking over. It was Mikey's plan, wasn't it? And Mikey's divorce.

"Your parents will call the police. It's what parents do. That's part of the panic you want — "

Mikey had an idea, then, of how to get her plan back in her own hands, and getting the glory of the adventure all to herself. "Why don't you just shut up," she said.

Margalo started to get angry, and turn away.

Good, Mikey said to herself.

Then there was a little wrinkling of Margalo's eyebrows, and a little narrowing of Margalo's eyes, and a little moving of Margalo's mouth into a pursed-up pruny thing.

Uh-oh, Mikey said to herself. She stretched her mouth wide, in a fake, innocent smile.

Margalo's face got blank, expressionless, and she stared right into Mikey's eyes to say, "Okay. If that's the way you want it. But you're making unnecessary mistakes just so you can stay the big boss lady. That's not overly smart, Mikey."

Margalo turned around, and walked away, and didn't even look back over her shoulder to see what Mikey would say next.

She couldn't have seen that anyway, Mikey thought. You didn't *see* what people said. You heard it. What was wrong with Margalo, anyway?

The trouble was, Margalo was people-smart. Mikey couldn't kid herself about that. Margalo got people to act the way she wanted them to, a lot of the time. Mikey could make things go the way she wanted, mostly, when it was all up to her. But this wasn't all up to her, and there were people in it.

So at lunch she sat at the end of the long table, with Margalo beside her. They didn't even try to nudge Gianette out of the spotlight. Gianette had the attention of the whole lunch table, with her information about Miss Brinson's boyfriend, her stories of the *belle-dame*'s voodoo spells, her complaints about the notes boys left in her cubby, and did they want to hear the worst ones? Gianette was talking away, being the center of attention, so Mikey could turn to Margalo and say, "Okay. You can help."

Margalo didn't pretend she wasn't interested and she didn't expect any apology, either.

It took three days to get a finished plan, because they quarreled about what to do, and also because they'd take a break from the work of planning and then see flaws they hadn't noticed before. "I can't believe I missed that," Margalo would say, and "I'm glad I thought of that," Mikey would say. When they had finished with it, they were both satisfied. "We're good," they said. "We're really good at this." The plan went into effect as soon as school got out, on Friday, October thirteenth.

On Friday, October thirteenth, they rode the bus to Mikey's stop, as usual. Margalo hid her sleeping bag in the bushes by the electric company's fenced-in transformer, where Mikey had already hidden hers early in the morning.

They went to Mikey's house, emptied the books from their backpacks onto her spare bed, and

Mikey took out the note they'd composed. "We've gone for a long walk," the note said. They set it out on the kitchen counter, where Mrs. Elsinger would see it and not even wonder, until dinnertime, where they were. This gave them plenty of time to get away.

Mikey carried a pack of cards. Margalo had a copy of *Grimms' Fairy Tales*. Those would keep them amused, if they needed amusement, if the weekend turned rainy. They could take turns reading aloud, or they could play games of gin rummy, for hours.

Mikey brought all of her money, almost forty-six dollars. "That's way too much," Margalo objected.

"What if we want to go to the movies?" Mikey argued.

"Dumb," Margalo pointed out.

They walked from Mikey's house to the Rite-Aid, where the bus would stop, and where there was a supermarket next door to the superpharmacy. Margalo stayed with the sleeping bags and backpacks while Mikey shopped for food. When they were discovered missing, they figured, people would try to remember seeing two girls. Not one girl, waiting for a bus with a sleeping bag, or one girl shopping for her family, getting slices of ham, slices of cheese, loaves of bread, boxes of Oreos and Fig Newtons, apples, bananas, oranges, and two big gallon jugs of water. Margalo had packed a flashlight and some matches. Mikey bought spare batteries at the market.

They'd never actually seen their destination, but they trusted Gianette — whom neither one of them trusted, "not as far as I could throw her," Mikey said, figuring even if she tossed the girl with all of her strength, Gianette wouldn't hit the ground more than four or five feet away — not to have lied about there being some isolated and uninhabited structure near her house. "A good liar," said Margalo, who knew about these things, "starts with the truth. So there must be a building of some kind there. Probably. Maybe just an old farmhouse, or a falling-down barn, but it'll be shelter."

The previous weekend, Mikey had ridden this bus route, from the Rite-Aid all the way to the city and then back. Her parents thought she was with friends at the mall; actually, her mother believed Mikey was meeting her boyfriend there and Mikey didn't correct that misconception. The bus ride to the city and back wasted a whole afternoon, but Mikey saw that there was only one trailer-park stop on the bus route. That had to be the one Gianette had mentioned.

So on Friday the thirteenth, their backpacks heavy with food, their sleeping bags under their arms, first Mikey, then Margalo — later, on the next bus, each of them just a girl traveling alone — rode out to the stop for Nottingham Forest Estates, which was two stops before the trailer-park stop. Mikey had to wait for the next long, silver bus to pull up to the stop. Three people got off, and one of them was Margalo.

They couldn't help grinning away at each other.

They entered Nottingham Forest Estates, in case anyone was watching them and remembered two girls and where they had gone. They went down Robin Hood Road, which was the main artery in, then turned left onto Little John Lane, where they cut through an unfenced yard and got back to the highway.

They couldn't help feeling pretty clever.

It was two or three miles down the road to the trailer park, and by the time they got there, Margalo was red in the face and tired. "Why'd we get off so far away?" she demanded.

Mikey wasn't tired. "You don't get as much exercise as I do, do you?" she asked.

"Next time we run away, remind me to get in shape first," Margalo answered, sarcastic.

They trudged on in front of the trailer park.

According to Gianette, their road turned off just beyond that.

"Do you see any big dogs?" Mikey asked.

"Do you think the fox was a lie too?"

The trailer park had two dirt streets running straight between three rows of trailers. They heard a couple of yapping dogs, but nothing that sounded dangerous, like a pinscher or a pit bull. They peered in among the trailers.

"Is that it?" Margalo asked.

Mikey looked to where she was pointing, a trailer in the center row. "That's a corgi," she said. "Or a dachshund, it's a dachshund. Or a short mutt."

They crossed slowly in front of the trailers, then turned and walked slowly down the road, looking into the yards.

"There," Mikey said.

Through the space between two trailers, they could see an unfenced dirt yard where a small reddish animal paced at the end of a rope, dragging its long tail. There was no mistaking it, once they had seen it. It had to be a fox, and wild. There was something about the *way* it moved, back and forth, crossing the yard, restless and purposeless. It reminded Mikey of a shark. "They say that sharks die if they stay still," Mikey said to Margalo.

They couldn't help stopping to stare at the fox.

"It's how sharks breathe," Margalo said. "They can't breathe unless they're moving."

"They move around even when they're asleep?"

"They must, if they have to, to breathe."

"Do you think he keeps pacing even when he's asleep?"

"I think he doesn't sleep. It could be a she," Margalo said. Then she added, "Wild animals are dangerous."

"We have to get going," Mikey said. "It can't be all that far now."

Two long curves down the road, they saw a little stone house ahead, on the left, near tall white gateposts. A driveway ran between the gates and across a field, then disappeared among trees.

Mikey and Margalo walked on by, as if they had no interest in this driveway, as if they had no idea who lived in that stone house by the gates, as if they weren't hoping — hard, and without saying anything — that Gianette wouldn't look out the window right then.

"Do you think she was telling the truth about it being a mansion?" Margalo asked.

"We're going to need to be pretty careful, not to be seen."

"I'd hate to think she wasn't lying."

"We'll cut back. This *has* to be it."

The woods beyond had NO TRESPASSING signs posted on the trees, and NO HUNTING signs. The two girls walked on along the road, until they came to a FOR SALE sign, a billboard. "Thirty-six acres, suitable for development. Zoned residential," the sign said. Mikey led the way through the woods until they came to the driveway again. When Mikey looked back along the driveway, she saw just a sliver of roof topped by a TV antenna. She didn't think they could be seen from the gatehouse.

"I can't stand it if she's telling the truth," Margalo announced, starting off up along the driveway. "If she only lies sometimes, even if she only lies most of the time, how am I supposed to *know* she's lying?"

The sun was getting lower in the sky. They came to another set of white gateposts, with a white wrought-iron gate sagging open between them. Ahead, they saw a low white building with some of its many windows boarded over. The driveway led right up to broad front steps.

Margalo hesitated just inside the gate.

"Come on," Mikey urged her. Mikey was looking forward to getting there, an entirely new place they'd never been and didn't know anything about.

Nobody but them knew where they were, and even they didn't know what was waiting for them. This was a total adventure.

The building stretched out long, with broad steps leading up to a boarded-over doorway. Cautiously they approached. Their sneakers muffled the sound of their footsteps as — cautiously — they walked along the front and around to the back.

None of the windows on the back side were boarded over, and some of them seemed to be doors.

Margalo and Mikey dropped their sleeping bags on the wide stones of a patio. Through a pair of French doors they saw a big, empty room. They shrugged off their backpacks and turned to the lawn. The lowering sun made everything look golden — even the red clay of the two tennis courts; even the gray stones of the patio glowed gold; even the brambles and shambledy lawns looked magical.

"I knew I couldn't stand it," Margalo said. "We better go home."

"What?" Mikey protested. "You can't *do* that to me! I'll kill you!"

Margalo looked at her. And looked at her. And

kept on looking at her, until Mikey finally had to say, "What's the matter with you?"

"You really don't get jokes, do you?" Margalo said.

"That was a joke? Not very funny," Mikey said. "Ha, ha," she said.

Margalo changed the subject. "This doesn't look anything like a house house. Do you think it used to be a hotel?"

Neither of them moved.

"I don't believe in ghosts," Mikey said.

"I don't believe in breaking and entering," Margalo said.

"What if it rains?" Mikey asked.

"That's different."

"What if it gets cold?" Mikey asked.

"We have sleeping bags. We're wearing sweaters and sweatshirts."

"What if I want to?" Mikey asked.

"This is the kind of place where there could be ghosts, if there were ghosts," Margalo said. "Especially if it was somebody's house, somebody rich. It's rundown now, but — Why don't you ask your mother to buy it? Then — No, listen, you could let us live in it for free, while you lived with us, and everybody'd be getting what they want." Then she turned to face Mikey. "Did you really mean that? About killing me. Could you kill some-body? I mean *me*, could you kill me?"

"Sure," Mikey said. "Probably. If I had to. I bet. Couldn't you?"

"Not you," Margalo said. "I'm not sure about anyone else, either."

Margalo seemed to be taking this as a serious question. Which, Mikey thought, it was, if it actually was a question.

"If I did," Margalo said, "I'd have to shut off part of my mind."

Mikey said, "I don't think I would. I think I'd just be angry and do it."

Margalo didn't answer. Mikey walked up to look through the windows into the big room.

Mikey got back to the point. "I think you *could* do it."

"I never said I couldn't," Margalo said. "I just said I'd have to shut off part of my brain."

Mikey turned around. "Can you do that? What part needs shutting off?"

They wandered around the outside of the build-ing, looking in windows and talking about brains, if they had particular sections for particular kinds of information, or thoughts, and if dreams were prophetic. The air grew chilly as they returned to the patio, with its French doors. Mikey went up to one of the doors and turned its knob.

The knob turned in her hand. Mikey pushed the door and it opened.

"How do you feel about just entering?" she asked Margalo. "Without any breaking?"

She had already stepped inside, into a big room where deep blue darkening sky showed through a fallen-down part of the roof. The wooden floor was stained and warped, but at one end of the room, under a solid roof, there was a stone fireplace big enough to stand up in. Its heavy stone chimney rose up through the ceiling. They should sleep here, inside, by the fireplace. "Let's bring our sleeping bags — "

Margalo had hesitated by the door. "It makes me nervous, Mikey."

"Not me. Isn't that why you came along? So I wouldn't be nervous?"

Margalo laughed, nervously, and explained, "It's different when you mess around with things people *own*. And the sign says no trespassing. But probably, even if we were caught, they wouldn't do more than tell our parents. And Aurora will be angry enough anyway, at me when she finds out. So, I guess, so what?"

"So, sew buttons," Mikey answered. She went past Margalo to get her backpack and sleeping bag.

When she turned around again, Margalo was inside the room, peering through a doorway beside the fireplace and asking Mikey, "Do you want to explore the rest of it?"

"I thought you were nervous," Mikey complained.

Margalo shrugged. "I am. But — it's exciting, too. It's even fun being a little afraid, like a roller coaster. Don't you want to explore?"

"Let's wait until tomorrow, when there'll be light."

"Besides," Margalo said, "if we want a fire, we have to gather some wood."

"For a fire?"

"We have a fireplace."

"Yes, but — "

"You don't want a fire?"

"Houses can burn down. With people in them."

"This is the ground floor," Margalo said.

"Do you promise to wake me up? If," Mikey said. She unrolled her sleeping bag a little ways away from the fireplace. Margalo set their food out against the wall beside the fireplace.

"I didn't know you were afraid of fires," Margalo said.

"I'm not afraid of them. I respect them. Sort of like being a little nervous about being caught trespassing," she reminded Margalo. "So let's get some wood."

They went into the woods beyond the tennis courts to find sticks and branches, dry leaves and grass. They made three trips, piling extra branches up beside the fireplace. When they had their fire going, they sat in front of it, making sandwiches, peeling oranges, drinking water, eating cookies, and talking. They kept the fire small. The windows grew dark.

They played gin rummy, for hours and hours, then took turns reading aloud to one another — "Hansel and Gretel" first, then "The Musicians of Bremen." Then they took off their shoes and slipped fully dressed into their sleeping bags. All around them, where they lay in the abandoned building, cozy in their sleeping bags despite their solitude, there was a deep silence.

There was a clear, black, empty silence spread out all around, except —

"Listen," Mikey whispered.

It might be a breeze, she thought, the slight rustling sound.

She felt Margalo go from sleepy to alert.

"You don't believe in ghosts — really — do you?" Margalo whispered.

Was there something outside on the patio? Was

that the scuffling sound of feet on flat stones? or something worse? Or some animal?

"We should have set booby traps," Mikey whispered. It was too late now. She wormed herself out of her sleeping bag and stood up, with only her socks to keep her feet warm.

October nights got pretty cold.

"There aren't any wild animals around here, are there?" Margalo whispered. "Why're you out of your sleeping bag? You can zip yourself in and hide. I mean, dangerous wild animals."

"What if I need to run?" Mikey padded on stocking feet over to the windows looking out over the patio. Margalo was right behind her. They stood side by side, trying to see into the darkness. There wasn't any wind at all. Then what was making that sound?

Margalo's hand grabbed at Mikey's arm at the same time that — peering out into starlit darkness — Mikey saw it.

A moving patch of light, about four feet above the ground, almost floating. It was almost a face, with two dark eyelike, pebblelike shapes close together at its top over a black circle like a howling mouth. The almost-a-face shone, shining out in the color of flesh in flames.

It approached the windows and floated back, as

if it was being carried along on some dark invisible current of air.

If there had been a moon, Mikey thought, she could have seen if this thing cast any shadows, and what shape the shadows took. But there was no moon.

"*Why* don't you believe in ghosts?" Margalo whispered.

The dim firelight showed two dark sleeping bags, which could have had people asleep in them.

Mikey whispered, "There would be too many, after all this time. We couldn't breathe, the air would be so crowded with them."

A thin noise entered the big living room, winding in through the broken windowpanes.

It was a thin, howling noise, like somebody being smothered to death.

The almost-a-face floated up close to the door and slid sideways.

"Ghosts don't make sense," Margalo whispered, agreeing.

The sound from outside grew fatter, humming and howling.

Mikey was getting suspicious.

Margalo stepped out toward the French doors, no longer trying to hide. She was a dark shadow running right toward the floating almost-a-face.

Almost running into it, and she was screaming.

Margalo's scream shrieked into the darkness all around them. She screamed once, and again. She screamed a third time, like the sound of a chain saw cutting the life out of a tree. She was clutching at her throat.

"Margalo?" Mikey called it out loud, almost right up to her now. A floating almost-a-face wasn't frightening, but Margalo's screams, and the way her fingers scratched at her throat, *that* scared Mikey.

Margalo fell down, smack onto the floor. One hand was at her throat and the other pounded on the floor. Her legs twitched, just a little.

"Margalo!" Mikey yelled. Mikey knelt down and yelled it again, right into Margalo's face. "Margalo!" The light was so bad, she could barely see Margalo's eyes.

They were open, she could tell that.

"You cut this out!" Mikey yelled. She held Margalo's shoulders down flat against the floor.

She had no idea why she did that.

She heard Margalo take a deep, raggedy breath. Then Margalo didn't breathe.

"Margalo?" she asked. A pulse, she needed to find a pulse. Girls not even twelve yet didn't have heart attacks. That was a scientific fact, or anyway, not heart attacks out of the blue. If Margalo had a heart condition, she'd have told Mikey, wouldn't she? Mikey hadn't known that Margalo was so afraid of ghosts. She should never have let Margalo come with her. "Margalo!" she yelled again.

Margalo took another rough breath. Her head tumbled to the side.

Children didn't just die like this.

Mikey was terrified. She was furious. She didn't know what to do, and she tried to find where Margalo's pulse would be — would have been — under the jaw. Mikey poked around with her forefinger and middle finger, trying to find the place where Margalo's pulse would be. If there was a pulse.

Margalo didn't move.

Suddenly a spotlight fell on Margalo, lying there with her head turned to one side. Her wide open eyes looked towards the fireplace but didn't see it.

Mikey looked up. "I knew it was you," she said.

Gianette had a flashlight in her hand, and her dark hair floated around her head like a storm cloud. Her clothing, sweater and skirt, was entirely dark blue.

"Is she dead? Death was the card she drew,"

Gianette said. She stood over Margalo's body, shining her flashlight down on Margalo's face.

"I tried to warn her," Gianette said, with a little smile.

Mikey's fingers had found the place where a pulse beat steadily in Margalo's neck. Okay, she thought. Then she wondered, How long could Margalo hold her breath like that? And, What was Margalo planning?

9.
Friday the Thirteenth, Part II

Mikey rose to her feet at the head of Margalo's prostrate body. Gianette stayed at Margalo's feet, but now she aimed her flashlight at Mikey. Gianette's eyes were black, huge. Her mean little mouth curved up, in a mean little smile. Her voice was full of suspicions and threats when she asked, "And now what will you do? Now you have murdered her."

"I didn't," Mikey said. In the first place, Margalo wasn't dead, which seemed like a basic requirement for murder. In the second place, Mikey wasn't about to get suckered into the horror-movie scene Gianette was working to produce. Mikey didn't know what Margalo had in mind, but she could wait and see. She said, "If anyone did, it was you. With your dumb ghost act."

"Who would believe I was here, if you told them so? No, no one. We have to bury her, and then you must truly run away."

"Who says I'm running away?" Mikey demanded. "And what are you doing here anyway?"

Gianette shone her flashlight around the room, not answering.

Anger rose up in Mikey, warming her, a good, friendly fury. She'd never invited Gianette St. Etienne into her life. She didn't like the girl just about as much as she ever hadn't liked anyone, Louis Caselli included. "Trying to scare us, sticking a stupid flashlight in your mouth, of all the little-kid tricks. And howling into it."

"Yet it was good enough. To frighten her," Gianette said, with a dramatic finger pointing downward. "To death," she whispered.

Margalo's body sat up. Her arms stuck stiff out in front of her. Her eyes were wide open. Margalo stared, and stared, right at Gianette's stomach.

Margalo's eyes were open, but she wasn't seeing anything.

Gianette edged back.

Mikey stayed where she was.

Margalo's arms dropped to her side. Her palms slapped down flat on the wooden floor.

She moved like some jointed puppet.

One at a time her legs bent back from the knees, lay flat along side of her body, heels close to her hips, her legs fencing in her hands.

She stared straight ahead.

Gianette started sliding away from Margalo's sightless glance, but she didn't take her eyes off of Margalo. Not for one second.

Margalo's hands rose up, then slapped palm down on the floor outside of her legs.

And she rose up.

Margalo rose up until she stood on her feet. Her arms snapped out straight in front of her again and she turned — like a weathervane, or a compass finding magnetic north — toward Gianette.

Mikey didn't know that Margalo was this good an actress. She hadn't even suspected it. Mikey was impressed. Also, she was having a really good time.

Gianette stepped backward, one step, two.

Margalo stepped forward, one step, two.

Gianette said to Margalo, "I am one of the protected ones," but she was swallowing hard as she spoke.

A voice spoke out of Margalo's mouth, a voice like the creaking of a door. "From the land of the dead."

Wow, Mikey thought. Oh, wow. She fought to keep her face blank, but she didn't really need to bother, since Gianette never looked away from Margalo. When Gianette held up her hands, to stop Margalo's relentless and robotlike approach, the flashlight clattered onto the floor.

"To claim the false pretender," creaked Margalo. "I am undead, the undead one. Never to die again."

"Spells protect me," Gianette said. She formed her two forefingers into a cross, holding them out in front of her face as if Margalo were a vampire. "I am protected by this cross."

"False pretender. False of spells. False of cross. You are," Margalo creaked, shuffling in slow motion closer to Gianette, so close her hands almost touched the girl, "no body, no one, no longer. No member of humankind."

The flashlight beam was shooting off into the darkness across the room, casting as much shadow as light on the scene.

Gianette fell to her knees, her dark head bent down like somebody asking a boon from the queen. "I have brought you a gift, better than myself," she said. "I have brought you this living body," and she raised her hand to point at Mikey. "This human, she is my gift to you. A gift from your true servant."

Gianette sounded as if she really thought she was talking to a zombie, not like someone playing a part.

But then Margalo didn't sound like someone playing a part, either.

"The human is yours to torment, and she is my gift to you. As I am, and ever will be, your true servant," Gianette said.

Margalo's arms fell down to her sides, and she spoke in her normal voice. "As you are, and ever will be, a total jerk."

Then she started laughing. Mikey laughed with her.

Mikey couldn't control her laughter. Her knees buckled and she had to sit down. Beside her, Margalo stayed on her feet, but both of them were howling and howling with laughter.

Gianette scrambled up to her feet, smiling. "But I was never deceived. You think you have tricked me, but I have tricked you." Then she pretended she was laughing, a pretty bad piece of pretend laughing, with fake shaking of shoulders, and *ha-ha-ha*s clunking down like falling marbles.

Margalo had caught her breath. She picked up the fallen flashlight and shone it where it would illuminate Mikey's face. "That was fun," she said. "That was really fun."

"Yes, it was," Gianette horned in.

"So, what do you want?" Mikey started to ask, standing up again, then being seized by the severe giggles at the memory of Margalo, creaking away, with her arms out straight. With that memory it was hard to concentrate on disliking Gianette. "What *are* you doing here? What do you want?"

"Give me my flashlight," Gianette said. Margalo handed it to her and she shone it first at Mikey, then at Margalo, and then she told them, "I knew where you were. I suspected, and I watched, and I saw you."

"Big deal," Mikey said. She knew Gianette hadn't yet gotten to her point, whatever that was.

"But I spect you don't want anyone to know where you are hiding out. I spect, specially your parents," she said to Mikey. "I'm not sure what part you have in this," she said to Margalo, "and I am not interested in you. Not for the moment," she added.

Gianette was like some movie villain, holding

her flashlight like a gun, trying to scare them with threats. It made Mikey want to grab the flashlight and whonk her on the ear with it.

On second thought, the flashlight was too small. Mikey would rather just punch Gianette. Even though she was much smaller than Mikey, a rap in the gums was the best response to this Nazi interrogator imitation.

Gianette smiled, Kevin Spacey playing a Nazi colonel interrogating a member of the French Resistance. "Tell me: What is it you hope to get from your parents, by this running away?"

"None of your business."

"Then perhaps," Gianette said, in charge now, "you wouldn't want me to telephone from my house and reassure them. They would be glad to know that you are safe."

Mikey didn't say anything.

"I think I had better go to do that, because by this hour they will be stremely worried and it will relieve them to know where you have hidden yourself."

Gianette turned to leave the room through the French door she had left open when she came in.

Margalo said, "Close the door behind you, please."

Gianette turned around again and took a step toward them. Whenever she moved, the beam of light moved also, sweeping through the darkness, and now it swept back toward Mikey and Margalo as Gianette turned to face them.

"I go back to my grandmother's house, to telephone."

She turned around, took another step, turned back to shine the light on Mikey. "Unless . . ."

Mikey said not a word, although by now she had figured Gianette's game out. Margalo also kept quiet.

Gianette waited.

"Unless," Gianette finally said, "you were to pay me for my silence?"

Mikey had already made up her mind. "Five dollars."

"So little?"

"Take it or leave it," Mikey said, in her own gangster voice.

Gianette shone the flashlight into Mikey's face for a while, then gave in. "All right."

Mikey dug into her pocket and pulled out bills. She counted out five ones.

Gianette counted them also. Then she smiled at both of them, a threatening little smile. "*Au revoir*," she said, and ran out the door. As she crossed the threshhold, she clicked off the light and disappeared into the night.

The dark silence closed in around them again. It was so dark that the dim light from the dying fire was enough to see by.

" *'Au revoir'*?" Mikey echoed. "She's such a twitface. . . . Why does everybody like her?"

"She'll be back," Margalo said. "Blackmailers come back for more, everybody knows that."

"She's really creepy," Mikey said. "She's almost not like a kid at all. She's more like a grown-up, don't you think? If she hadn't had money stolen, I'd suspect her of being the person who was stealing money at school. Wouldn't you?"

"You know," Margalo said thoughtfully, "if it were me, I'd say I was robbed too, to divert suspicion. That would be a smart thing to do, making yourself look like one of the victims while you're actually the perp." She had always wanted to use that word, *perp*, in a sentence, as if she were a TV policewoman.

They got back into their sleeping bags but were too revved up to sleep, so they discussed the possibility of robbing a bank if, instead of running out to the street to a getaway car, you pretended to be one of the robbery victims. You'd have to lie down on the floor. "Or you could pretend you'd been trapped in the bathroom during the robbery," Mikey said. "But where would you hide all the money?"

Margalo had lots of ideas about that. Mikey wasn't surprised.

In the morning, strangeness and sunlight and bird songs woke Mikey up early. The air was cool but she was warm in her sleeping bag. She turned her head. Margalo was staring at her. Mikey couldn't stop the smile from spreading over her face.

Outside, a light fall mist hovered over the overgrown lawns, shimmering like some magical veil, as the sunlight grew brighter.

But some of the birds were crows and some of the bird songs were caws. Everything wasn't perfect after all, and that was good news. Perfect made Mikey nervous.

Mikey and Margalo separated, to go to the bathroom in private bushes, then sat on the edge of the patio to eat breakfast. A sandwich, an orange, some water: "How long do you think it'll be before we get sick of sandwiches?" Margalo asked.

"I'm already bored of ham and cheese," Mikey said.

"Too bad for you."

They ate, and listened to the Saturday morning.

"It's good the sun's out," Margalo said after a while.

"Maybe I'll have plain cheese for lunch," Mikey said.

"We should get more wood, first thing, for the fire tonight. We should have that taken care of, before anything else."

"And plain ham for supper," Mikey said. "There's no way we could make our beds if we even wanted to," she announced happily.

They peeled the oranges and ate them slowly, one section at a time. The quiet was soft, friendly.

"I wonder," Margalo said.

"Wonder what?"

"Do you realize, there are no grown-ups? Not even if we yelled for help? We're really on our own."

"Well, duh," Mikey said.

"Do you think this is what being grown up will feel like, when we are?"

"You mean, having nobody older around telling you things to do?"

"Or knowing," Margalo said. "Knowing what has to be done."

"Telling you who you are, what you're like," Mikey said.

"I wonder."

"I wish you'd stop saying that," Mikey complained. "It's boring the way you say 'I wonder' like that, and I have to say 'What?' "

Margalo pretended to ignore what Mikey said. "I was going to say," she said, "that I'd like to be as clear in my own mind as you are, about what you think, but I bet you wish sometimes you had someone like Aurora — whatever you sometimes say about her — so I wonder if, if you're friends with someone, you'll always be a little jealous, too. Not that much, but still."

"Where did *that* idea come from?" Mikey demanded.

"My head."

"You think too much. Did anyone ever tell you that? Besides me, I mean."

Margalo thought long and seriously about that. Finally she shook her head and grinned at Mikey, *Gotcha.* "What'll we do today?"

Mikey looked out over the lawn. There were five hundred things she wanted to do, but she wasn't sure she wanted to move. The day lay before them like a still pond. She didn't want to disturb the waters, not just yet. She pretended she was thinking but really she was just sitting still, floating on the glassy stillness, just being there, just herself all by herself.

Margalo sat just as quiet beside her.

After a while Mikey decided, "I'll teach you tennis."

They had their faces turned up into the sun. Margalo had taken off her socks and Mikey was thinking of doing the same.

"We didn't bring racquets. Or balls," Margalo objected.

"That doesn't matter."

"There's no net up on the courts," Margalo said.

"We'll pretend. It'll be almost the same. I can teach you how to score, because that's hard."

"Okay," Margalo said. "I think this year I'm going to run for class treasurer, not president. Or maybe vice president."

"You just don't want to run against Ira."

"What I don't want, Mikey, is to lose."

"And I'm your campaign manager," Mikey reminded Margalo, to show her that she still remembered the deal they had made last year.

"Actually," Margalo said.

Mikey opened her eyes to look at Margalo.

"Yes?" she asked, already half angry.

"The thing is, I never know how people are going to react to you," Margalo said.

"I thought you were so good at figuring people out."

"The thing is," Margalo said, "not everybody likes you."

Mikey just laughed out loud.

And Margalo joined in. "So I'd rather run my own campaign," Margalo said. "If that's okay with you."

"Sure," Mikey said. Running Margalo's political campaign wasn't anything she wanted to do anyway, and it would have taken time away from soccer, too.

And besides, she thought, she might not even be around for the election. If her parents didn't get back together about their disappeared daughter, then they could decide to split up, any day they wanted, and there Mikey would be — out of school, out of town, out of luck.

Mikey jumped up. Energy filled her as if someone had started up an internal-combustion engine in her stomach. She didn't know what to do with the idea that her whole life could be changed, any morning, anytime somebody decided, without her being able to do anything about it. She tried to swallow the idea down and keep it down. But she couldn't. So she told it to Margalo. "I could have to move away, anytime."

"That would really suck," Margalo said, and "I'd hate it," Mikey said.

"Do you think running away is going to work?" Mikey wondered.

"Well," Margalo said, "nobody wants to be the kind of parents whose kids run away from home. Because people might say you're a bad parent, and your mother would hate that. Even if the kid is really a horrible person, people always suspect things about the parents."

"Well, sometimes they're right to," Mikey pointed out.

"But nobody wants to be embarrassed in public. Nobody wants everybody talking about them. Especially your mother."

"They might just blame each other for me, like they do for everything else," Mikey said.

"They might," Margalo agreed. "Tell only will time," she announced, like she was Yoda talking to Luke Skywalker.

Mikey said, "I guess you could say that," sarcastically. "So let's get going."

Weeds and grasses had grown up through the cracks in the asphalt of the tennis courts, and the painted white lines had faded to pale gray. There was no net between the two posts. Margalo waited while Mikey took stock of the situation. "Okay," Mikey said.

"Okay," Margalo said, going along with it.

"Here's your racquet." Mikey mimed passing Margalo a tennis racquet and Margalo mimed taking it by the handle. "There's forehand" — Mikey demonstrated with her own invisible racquet — "and backhand. You want a two-handed backhand, for power. And" — she tossed an invisible ball up into the air and whipped down on it — "there's the serve."

"Forehand," Margalo demonstrated, "backhand," she demonstrated again, "and serve."

"Now go stand across the court from me," Mikey said. "We'll play."

"You really like being in charge, don't you?" Margalo said. "What if I wanted to be on that side? Because of the sun in my eyes," she pointed out.

Mikey had the answer to that. "We switch sides on odd games."

"You know what I mean," Margalo said.

"How else can I teach you?" Mikey pointed out. "If you won't let me be the teacher."

"I don't mind if you're the teacher," Margalo called, jogging to her place at the back of the court opposite Mikey. "I just don't want to be the student."

"I'm going to serve, into that inside box, the one on your right," Mikey said. "You stand about at the middle to receive."

She served. It was an ace. "Fifteen–love," she said.

"How'd you get fifteen so fast?" Margalo objected.

"Now cross to the other side. I'm serving into that box. The serve alternates back and forth between the boxes. Fifteen is like, one."

"Then why not say one?" Margalo asked.

Mikey served a second ace. This one Margalo swung at. "Thirty–love," Mikey called. "The server's score is always given first. Cross back."

"I know."

Mikey's third serve was also destined to be an ace, but Margalo felt that she had returned it, with a forehand. Mikey pointed out that the serve had gone to Margalo's backhand. Margalo groaned. "That makes it forty-five–love, right?"

"No, forty–love."

"Mikey," Margalo objected.

"It goes fifteen, thirty, forty, game," Mikey said. "I'm winning this game."

"Not yet," Margalo grinned, and swung wildly

at Mikey's serve. Mikey watched the invisible ball go up, up, and over the high rusty fence.

"Out," she called. "One game to love. Now we switch sides."

"Love is zero, right?" Margalo said. "Do you think they did that for a symbol?"

"I think they did it for French," Mikey told her. "My father explained it to me. Are you going to serve, or what?"

Being a beginner, Margalo had trouble serving. Also, when her serve was in, it was so weak that Mikey killed it. She won the second game easily.

By the third, Margalo was getting cross. Anger improved her game, and she finally scored a point. "Thirty–fifteen," Mikey admitted, then "Thirty-all," then "Forty–thirty," and they arrived at deuce.

"What?" Margalo was getting a little red in the face from the crosscourt exchanges and general irritation.

"Deuce," Mikey repeated patiently. She explained, "Now one of us has to win two points in a row to win the game. If I win the first one, it's advantage in. If you do, it's advantage out. Or ad," Mikey said, and served. "Ad in," she called.

"My shot was in," Margalo argued.

"It hit the top of the net," Mikey argued.

"Then it skidded over the top," Margalo argued.

"Then it went out," Mikey argued. "Just out. You have to let me call the balls on my own side of the court."

"Okay, but I'm not going to let you win," Margalo said. "I don't care if it's an invisible game, with illogical ways of keeping score, and you keep changing the rules — "

"I never changed the rules. I'm playing by the rules."

" — I'm still not going to just let you win," Margalo said. "Even if you are a better player."

"Illogical? What's illogical about it?" Mikey demanded.

They gathered wood for the evening's fire and explored inside the building. It had been a hotel, they decided. It was dangerously decrepit, between rotted-out and fallen beams and rotted-out and fallen floorboards and rotted-out and fallen-in roof sections. They had sandwiches and fruit and water for lunch, with a few cookies, and wondered if Gianette could be trusted to keep their secret.

Margalo thought she could. "She likes having something on us. If she tells, she won't have it anymore."

Mikey tended to agree with that, and observed, "You know, if she's the one who's been stealing, that means she went into Miss Brinson's purse. That takes nerve."

"Gianette's got plenty of nerve," Margalo said.

"She didn't even care if you'd died last night," Mikey said.

"Neither did you," Margalo pointed out.

"I didn't care because you weren't dead. She thought you were."

"She didn't even sound sorry," Margalo said.

"I was watching her and she wasn't. What should we do to get back at her for blackmailing us?"

Margalo jammed the last of her banana into her mouth and shook her head. Mikey had to wait until she swallowed. Then Margalo explained, "Someone like Gianette, it's not like Louis Caselli, where he wins, then we win, then he gets even again and then we really clobber him. Gianette's dangerous, because she's playing for keeps. I think she's the kind of crazy — no, I'm serious, if she knew how to do it she'd want to blow up the whole world. She doesn't care what she does; all she cares about is getting away with it."

"Getting caught's not so bad." Mikey spoke from experience.

"I bet you don't win out over Gianette more

than once," Margalo said. "I bet if you do, something really bad will happen."

"Like what? A magic spell?"

"My guess is . . . Gianette will — Like the way she's trying to put the blame for stealing on Louis, and that's the kind of thing that when it's on your school record, people always read your record, so you'd never get away from it. It's like ruining his whole life, and she doesn't care. It's like putting a tattoo on him."

"Tattoos can be lasered off," Mikey argued.

"You know what I mean."

Mikey did, even if she wasn't about to admit it. "I don't want to give her all of my baby-sitting money."

"How much do you have?"

"Two more fives, a few ones, some change. I guess it might be worth it, if I have to, to keep her quiet. I can always earn more." Mikey realized something: "I know how to earn money."

"Dunnh," Margalo answered.

"So I can always earn money," Mikey announced.

"Dunnh, dunnh," Margalo said.

"I don't even need them to give me an allowance," Mikey announced. "If you work, then you can be independent. Margalo? What kind of work do you think I should do? I mean, later, when I'm out of school." Margalo knew her pretty well, and was pretty smart, too. "What job do you think I'd be good at?"

They talked about jobs, and if Mikey could be a professional athlete, although there weren't that many fields for women professional athletes, and for two of those Mikey was already pretty late for starting. They wondered if being good at figuring out what people were up to meant that Margalo would make a good therapist, or if she'd have more fun being a detective. Mikey wasn't surprised to hear that Margalo wanted to make a lot of money when she had a job.

"I'm going to try to get baby-sitting jobs," Margalo announced. "The supermarket has a bulletin board."

"People advertise in the newspaper," Mikey added. She knew she should offer to ask her mother, but she didn't want to give up any jobs that might come to her. Margalo might need money more than Mikey, but Mikey needed the independence.

Then they decided to go for a walk. Playing it safe, Mikey put a five-dollar bill on the patio, weighted down with a rock. They hid their backpacks and sleeping bags in bushes beyond the tennis courts, and took the long way around to the road, so even if somebody in the little house by the gates was looking, she wouldn't see them. Just in case Gianette was as bad as they could imagine she would be, if she was as bad as they suspected.

Mikey chose the route. She let them walk on the road, but ducked into the woods whenever she heard a car. Margalo just followed her example. It was like a hide-and-seek game, except real. They didn't know what would happen if the police actually found them. In stories and movies, on TV and according to what parents said, the policemen would take them back to the police station and give them ice cream while they waited for their frantic parents to come claim them. But Mikey didn't exactly believe in stories, movies, TV, or parents. For a while, walking along, she and Margalo discussed that. "Did you used to believe them? Before they started getting divorced, I mean, because you always had two. I only always had Aurora."

"But you trust her," Mikey pointed out.

"Sort of," Margalo said. "She'd never leave me behind. But she'd never leave any kid behind. It's not just me."

"Would Steven leave kids?" Mikey asked.

Mikey was enjoying this talking. It was almost as interesting as doing something.

Margalo was telling her, "I don't know. He got custody of his kids, after his divorce, so he wouldn't leave his own kids. But I'm not sure about the rest of us."

"I think probably he wouldn't," Mikey decided. They were coming up on the trailer park, which was her destination, and she instructed Margalo, "Look, but pretend you're not looking, because I bet we can free that fox. Wouldn't you like to? Tomorrow, before we go home and get in trouble and find out what's going to happen. Look at it, tied up there. Can you think of a plan? Do you think Gianette was lying about the vicious dogs in here?"

Margalo walked along beside her. "I always start out as if she's lying."

"Do you think she is this time, too?"

"Wait, I'm looking. Wait."

Mikey waited.

After a while Margalo decided, "Probably there can't be vicious dogs, or at least not loose, because look at all the children. And swing sets and wading pools, bikes in yards. It's Saturday afternoon, I know, but still — you can't have vicious dogs around all these kids. Can you see how the fox is tied up?" she asked. "We don't have a knife, do we? And aren't wild animals — wild? I mean, dangerous?"

"I don't want to just leave it here," Mikey said. She hadn't realized until she said it that the fox actually did matter to her. "They never give me even a jackknife for Christmas. They talk like I've asked them for an Uzi."

"We can't be the only ones who want it freed, and it's still there," Margalo pointed out.

The fox paced back and forth, its long tail drooping. It paced as if it hoped to walk itself to death, and soon.

"It's tied on a rope," Mikey said. "If I had a knife, we could cut it."

"You can untie a rope, if you could keep the fox from biting."

"Put something over its head, a sweater. Haven't you seen that in movies? When the barn is burning down, they put cloths over the horses' heads to keep them from panicking, so they can lead them out. If an animal can't see . . ." But Mikey didn't know what the end of that idea was.

"Do you think if it can't see the danger, the danger might as well not exist? I mean, literally see. Do you think," and Margalo was off on one of her wilder ideas, "if a person closes her eyes to danger, she'll be better at getting out of it?"

"The horses don't always get out of the barn," Mikey reminded her.

"If you had a knife, we could be sure to get the fox free," Margalo said. "We could do it tomorrow, on our way to the bus. But we don't have a knife."

"We could still try," Mikey said.

"Try to get a knife?" Margalo asked. Mikey was about to punch her one in the shoulder for being so dumb, but she looked at Margalo's face and saw that it was a joke.

When they got back to the derelict hotel, the five-dollar bill was gone. "Gone to the mall" was Margalo's guess.

"Think she'll be back tonight for more?" Mikey asked.

Mikey watched closely while Margalo decided what she was going to answer to that question. Mikey waited because she thought probably Gianette had been invited to Linny's boy-girl party tonight, the one Mikey had heard about. She had assumed that Margalo, also, was not on the guest list, but now she wondered.

Finally, "I don't think so," Margalo said.

"Good."

They stood there, with nothing to do, looking down across the lawn.

"Want to play more tennis?" Mikey suggested. The great thing about a pretend tennis game was that every shot she made turned out as good as she hoped. In her imagination, she played like Pete Sampras.

Margalo asked, "Did you hear about Linny's party? I wasn't asked either."

"I wouldn't have wanted to go anyway," Mikey said.

"Do you think we're immature?"

"I don't care," Mikey said. The idea of dancing in a darkened room pounding with loud music, hoping some boy would ask you to dance, try to hold your hand . . . Hold your hand! What was that supposed to prove? Or try to kiss you, wanting boys to like you — those ideas made her bored and angry. They made her want to punch out any boy who came anywhere near her, to be sure he didn't get the wrong idea. "We're not even twelve, only almost. We don't have to behave like teenagers yet."

"I care," Margalo admitted.

"If she'd asked you, would you have gone?" Mikey wondered.

"Probably."

"So you do want to go to boy-girl parties?"

"No. But I want to be asked, and I want people to know I've been asked. If I went, I'd just stand around, nobody would — If I went, I'd have been sorry I was there, all night long."

"So it's a good thing you weren't asked," Mikey told Margalo. "So let's play a set of tennis," she suggested again, and offered, "I'll let you win this time."

10.

Home Again, Home Again, Jiggity Jog

Mikey left a nickel set out on the patio, as a sarcastic final blackmail payment to Gianette. This was Sunday morning. They rolled up their sleeping bags, put on their backpacks, and started for home. That had always been the plan, for Mikey to return in the middle of the afternoon.

"That gives them time to yell at you, then get over it," Margalo had explained. "So nobody goes to bed angry. The angry you go to bed with just gets worse," she explained. "Bigger," she explained.

On Sunday morning they didn't have to worry

about being seen, so they went right down the driveway and out through the gates onto the road, right past the little stone gatehouse. They walked slowly down the long road, as if they didn't want to be going home.

In fact, Margalo wasn't looking forward to all the trouble she'd be in once she got there. Mikey had some excuse for running away, but Margalo didn't, and any she made up wouldn't work with Aurora and Steven. But she'd known that before she started off. And she wasn't sorry, except she was sorry the good times were almost over and the bad times about to begin.

From the bus stop across the street from the trailer park they couldn't see the fox — but they were both waiting, and hoping, that something would happen. When something happened, then they could *do* something to free the fox. But Margalo didn't say anything, or do anything, and neither did Mikey, and pretty soon the bus came.

When they had gotten on the bus and sat to-gether — Mikey by the window — Margalo tried to plan for the emotional scene that awaited them. Mikey didn't buy Margalo's gloomy predictions. "I'm just showing them they can't get away with doing this to me."

Margalo didn't say anything.

Margalo didn't say anything in a way that made Mikey think there was a lot she would say, and could say.

"It's gone just like we wanted," Mikey said. "Except for the fox."

"Except for the fox," Margalo agreed. She knew it wasn't Mikey's fault that Aurora and Steven were going to hit the roof at her. She also knew she didn't have to worry about them hitting the roof *with* her, or hitting her with the roof. Since trouble couldn't arrive until it had arrived, she tried to forget that it was on its way.

"You don't have to sound so — If I'd known you wanted to try to free it, I'd have tried. You didn't say anything."

"Neither did you," Margalo answered.

They were silent and cross and filled with regret. Mikey wished she'd tried something, anything. If she'd just tried, she wouldn't feel so bad. She waited to see if Margalo would suggest getting off, and going back, and trying something. If Margalo did, Mikey'd do it in a minute.

But Margalo knew better. She didn't like it a bit, knowing better, and she was really sorry — for the fox, and for herself, too, because she wished she was the kind of person who would run in and fight the fox free. Mikey was that kind of person, but Mikey wasn't doing anything.

They sat and looked out the window.

"I wish I'd — "

"I wish you'd — "

"It isn't *right*. You don't keep wild animals tied up."

"I wish I had too, even if you didn't — "

"Next time I will. We will."

"We chickened out, didn't we, Mikey?"

"Never again," Mikey swore. "Deal?"

"Deal," Margalo promised.

They both hoped — although neither said so — that by giving their word to each other they'd have a better chance of keeping it.

They didn't see any unusual activity among policemen, out in their cruisers looking for runaways, not from the bus windows, and not walking back from the Rite-Aid. The bus driver didn't pay any particular attention to them. There were no notices, with photographs of missing girls, stapled up onto telephone poles, stuck up on the Rite-Aid bulletin board, taped onto store windows. "It's as if nobody even noticed," Margalo said. "Do you think your parents would just — not even notice?"

"They're busy being furious," Mikey promised her.

"Could they be so angry at each other they'd just — forget about you?" Margalo asked.

"They might," Mikey said. It was possible. She could imagine it. She would have liked to imagine it more clearly, because what she was imagining now was a lot less cheerful. If her parents had been in a car wreck driving to the police station, so upset and anxious about her that they drove badly, even worse than her mother usually did. If they had been killed, or were in the hospital, and if she hadn't run away this would never have happened.

But both of her parents' cars were in the garage, and there wasn't even anything that might have been an unmarked police vehicle parked on the street. The house looked like Sunday afternoon as usual.

"This is weird," Mikey said to Margalo.

"Weird," Margalo agreed.

They dropped their sleeping bags and backpacks by the front door. Mikey knew that it was her house, so she would have to go in first and find out what was waiting for them. She turned the handle and pushed, but the door wouldn't open. The door was locked.

She'd been locked out of her own house.

Even as she was leading Margalo around back,

almost running, Mikey was thinking that this might make things easier. Simpler, anyway. If they could just write her off, or forget her . . . How could they just forget her? They couldn't do that to her! As if she were nobody, some nobody, just some kid not their responsibility. At least, until she was eighteen. But on the other hand, her life would be a lot simpler without her parents around, especially the way they'd been acting recently. Ruining her life.

The back door was locked too, but her father sat at the kitchen table. He had the Sunday paper spread out all around him, on the table, on the floor, and when she knocked —

Mr. Elsinger looked glad for about one tenth of a second, and then he cleared all expression off of his face. Blank-faced, he got up and opened the door. He held the screen door open for them. "Lost your key?" he asked Mikey, but not as if it mattered if she had.

Mikey had put her key, on its red ribbon, out on top of her bureau. She had left it out in plain sight, on purpose. She had wanted them to think she never planned to come back. She guessed, maybe it served her right if they hadn't even noticed.

But it really made her angry that they hadn't

even noticed. She didn't answer her father.

"Have a good sleepout?" Mr. Elsinger asked, barely curious.

Mikey looked at Margalo and then turned back to her father, about to deny it, when he added in a serious voice, "Your mother wants to talk to you. You two wait in the den. She's upstairs, in the tub, having a soothing soak. I'll tell her you're back."

Mrs. Elsinger kept Mikey and Margalo waiting for a long time, although not as long as it felt to the two girls, sitting on the sofa, facing the blank TV screen. Mr. Elsinger did not wait with them.

"What do you think — ?" Mikey asked in a low voice.

Margalo shrugged, shook her head.

"They don't seem too worried," Mikey said. "Or shocked." She had better face the facts: There had been no calling of police, no telephoning other homes, no panicked posting of photographs, no sleepless nights.

Probably, they were glad to have her gone.

Leaving them in peace, for once.

Well, she'd liked it better without them around, too. Including her in their miseries and their quarrels. Making her think if she changed, then they'd change their minds about what they were doing.

Taking her own life away from her, making her life be about them.

"It's only six years until you're eighteen," Margalo reminded Mikey. "Maybe one of them will marry someone you like. It's not so bad being a stepchild."

"You've got Aurora," Mikey pointed out.

"That's not my fault," Margalo pointed out.

"That's not what I mean," Mikey said.

"It's not like I have her all to myself," Margalo said. "I don't feel sorry for you, Mikey."

"I'm not asking you to."

"You could have fooled me."

It felt good to be getting angry, even at Margalo. "Big deal, Miss Always Perfect."

"Ms.," Margalo said. "Call me Ms., Ms. Always Perfect."

Mikey could recognize a joke when she heard it, even if it stunk. "I'll call you Ms. Bad Joke. Ms. Not As Funny As She Thinks."

"*Notas* for short, right? I always wanted a nick-name," Margalo said.

So they were smiling, and not particularly anxious, and feeling only a little guilty, when Mikey's parents came into the room. Mikey's mother sat down in an armchair, facing them. Mikey's father sat down in another armchair, also facing them. The armchairs were on either side of the TV screen, which also faced them.

It was like a police interrogation. The TV would be the chief of police, because it was in the middle.

Mrs. Elsinger thought she was the chief. She stared at both of them for a while, and finally said, "Well, Mikey. This trick about takes the cake. I can never trust you again."

"Patty," Mr. Elsinger said. "I thought we agreed that — "

"I'm not going to let you spoil her like this, Anders. And as for you, Margalo Epps, I'm very disappointed in you. I can never have you in my house again."

Margalo sat very still. Sometimes the best thing was to sit still and let whatever people were going to say or do get said or done. Sometimes if you said or did something yourself, you would set people off and make things worse. Margalo didn't move.

"Don't be ridiculous, Patty."

"Are you calling me ridiculous?" Mikey's mother demanded.

"I just meant, that's so extreme. They only — "

"Don't go soft on me now, Mr. Cornpuff." She turned to Mikey again, like a fireman with a hose, hosing Mikey down with her anger. "How could you do this to me? What if I'd called the police? It would have been in the newspapers, and everybody would have known what you did to me. Not to mention the waste of police man-hours. It was very selfish, Mikey. Even for you."

"Patty. She's upset. Haven't you listened to what Dr. Taylor's been telling us? It's hard on her, getting divorced."

"It's hard on me and you don't see me running away from home, do you?"

Mikey's father didn't say anything. So Mikey did: "What about all that time you spend at the health club?"

"You always knew where I was. I work hard, I deserve some relaxation, and you could always reach me. I thought better of you, Margalo. I thought you'd be a better friend."

Margalo sat very still.

Mikey's father tried again. "We talked this over, Patty. We talked to Dr. Taylor, after that girl came, and we gave her her money. Yesterday morning, too, we talked it all over again, and you agreed. You said you agreed. No recriminations. You said you understood. You said you didn't blame her."

"I didn't mean it," Mikey's mother answered. "And neither should you, Anders." She turned back to Mikey. "Do you realize what we've had to put up with? Your little friend smacking her lips over us, smirking, butter wouldn't melt in her mouth. She enjoyed seeing how embarrassed I was. Of course, when she first got here, how was I to know she was selling information? She made us look like a pair of fools, Anders, don't kid yourself."

"Gianette?" Margalo asked. "Gianette came here?"

"She blackmailed me, too," Mikey told her parents. "How much did you pay her?"

"The first time? Or the second?" Mikey's mother asked. "I don't know how you could introduce someone like that into our lives. Twenty dollars, each time. We had to know where you were. I don't know what your little plan was, but I can assure you, it didn't work."

Mikey wasn't about to argue with that.

"We could have come to get you at any time, but we let you stay. Let you see how you liked running away."

Mikey was about to tell her mother how she'd liked it, just fine thank you, when her father horned in. "Margalo? What time are your parents coming to get you?"

"Sometime mid-afternoon, they said. It's a four-hour drive," she told him. She looked right at him when she answered his question and pretended Mrs. Elsinger wasn't even in the room.

"I think we had better ask you to wait for them outside," Mrs. Elsinger said. "I'm not suggesting that it was you who put Mikey up to this trick, or that you're in cahoots with that dreadful smarmy child, to split the profits with her."

"You don't know anything," Mikey told her mother. "There's a fox," she said. "A wild fox. They're keeping it tied up."

"Don't try to change the subject. I hope you're planning on being punished, Mikey."

"It just paces, at the end of its rope. All day long," Mikey said. "It doesn't even have grass."

"I thought we agreed that we needed to explain things and make them clearer to her," Mikey's father said.

"*I'm* trying to explain something," Mikey said, talking louder than either one of them. "They can't do that — tying a wild animal up like that. On a rope."

"It's none of your business what other people do," Mikey's mother told her.

"In a trailer park. It's in a trailer park, isn't it, Margalo?"

"Yes," Margalo said. "She's right," Margalo said, looking first at Mikey's father, then at

Mikey's mother. "We wanted to set it free."

"That is irrelevant," Mikey's mother announced. "You can't get out of being held responsible for what you choose to do, and the results of your choices. I hope you know that. If not, Mikey, you better learn it, fast. You're grounded, for a month. Your allowance is cancelled, for a month, and I'm thinking of asking you to pay me back the money that horrible child took from me."

"It's not about the money," Mikey's father said. "What's wrong with you, Patty?"

"But we couldn't because I don't have a knife," Mikey insisted. "You never let me have one. I asked, last Christmas, and the Christmas before, too, but you probably don't remember. If I'd had a knife, we could have cut the rope and set it free. Couldn't we have, Margalo?"

"Yes," Margalo said. "We could have."

"It's not as if we don't have enough money," Mikey's father said. "You sound like the money is all that matters."

"Now you're complaining because I'm capable of earning good money?" Mikey's mother asked. "No wonder I fell in love with someone else. And you, young lady," she switched the subject to Margalo, "I want you out of my house. As of now."

Mikey's father had stood up. "Why didn't you tell me you didn't love me?" he asked Mikey's mother. "That makes everything easy. There's no point in staying married if you don't love me," Mikey's father said.

"That fox shouldn't be there," Mikey insisted. "They can't do that to the fox."

Mikey's father promised her, "I'll do something about it."

"What can *you* do?" Mikey's mother demanded.

"I can make phone calls."

"You can't even do anything with your own daughter. She just ran away on us, don't you understand? It was sheer luck that we found out right away what she was doing and where she was, or can you imagine how frightening it would have been? She ran away to make us do what she wants. Get that through your thick skull. You think she cares about a fox? Mikey? Not likely, just as unlikely as that you can do anything to help the animal. You can't even control your daughter, Anders."

"I don't want to be controlled," Mikey said.

"At least," Mikey's father said, "I can control myself. Why don't you two girls both go outside and wait for Margalo's mother and father."

"Stepfather," Mikey's mother corrected him.

"And they're *my* beds," Mikey told them both. "*Mine.* You gave them to me when Nana died."

Margalo and Mikey sat on the curb with their legs sticking out into the road. They sat there for a long time without saying a word to each other.

The sunlit air was warm. The shady air was chilly. They kept in the sunlight.

Finally Mikey spoke. "I'm not sorry."

Margalo answered slowly, "Except it didn't work."

"No," Mikey agreed.

Margalo asked, "Are you sorry it didn't work?"

Mikey said, "It never would have worked. Gianette ruined any chances we had."

"But Mikey? Didn't you think — when they were talking — if I'd run away on Aurora and Steven — "

"I'll get her."

"Listen, Mikey, I never thought about it before, but one night would be long enough. Even for *your* parents. To really scare parents. Or even a couple of hours. A whole weekend was too long," Margalo said.

"We'll never know now what might have happened. All because of her."

"Unless you hate your parents. I mean, really and truly hate them. You don't, do you?"

"No. Why should I hate them? I'm just angry because — they're not thinking about me at all. Just about themselves. I know," Mikey said, interrupting Margalo even though Margalo had never even thought of giving voice to her thought, "I know. I'm doing the same thing, but — I get to be the child, don't I? That means I can be childish, doesn't it? And childish means selfish, when grown-ups call you that," she concluded.

"It was still too much, too long," Margalo said.

Mikey tried to think of arguments against that. "But," she said, but that was as far as she could get. "I guess you're right. I'm not going to apologize," she announced.

"I was just thinking, that was a flaw in the plan," Margalo said. "I thought I'd thought of everything, but I hadn't."

They were silent again. A couple of cars drove by and didn't stop.

"You know, Gianette did us a favor," Margalo said.

"You're not going to talk me into that," Mikey said.

"Good," Margalo said. She drew in her legs, wrapped her arms around her knees, and asked, "What're you going to do to her?"

"The way I feel, I'll beat her up. Kick her down. Beat her up again."

"Smart, Mikey, really smart."

"I don't care if it's smart."

"And," Margalo pointed out, "everyone will be on her side, if you do that, because she's popular. And, she'll look like the innocent victim, while you're the big bully."

"She's not that much shorter than I am."

"Can't you think of something less obvious?"

"Like what? Nuke her?"

"Can't you keep your temper long enough to follow a plan? You could sort of run into her, as if it was an accident, push her stuff onto the floor. You could step on her feet and trip her."

"That's not the same as punching her. Knocking her down and jumping on her. With both feet. Wearing boots."

"Yeah, but it'll upset her more. Because — if she trips, or falls, she'll look clumsy. And if she blames you, she'll look like a whiner. And — listen to this, Mikey, this is great — what I'll do is, I'll tell her how much I admire her. No, listen, at the lunch table, sometime when there are people around, I'll tell her how much I admire the way she got away with stealing from all those people, even a teacher, and getting everyone to think Louis did it. I'll praise her for being so clever about pretending she was robbed, too. It has to work, because — whether they believe me or not — people will start to wonder about her." Margalo was getting enthusiastic about this idea. "And if we tell them about the blackmail — "

"I don't want to," Mikey said.

"You need a good offense," Margalo said. "And so do I, because we made a fool of her. She'll be out for revenge."

Mikey turned and smiled at Margalo, a smile that was practically laughing. "That was fun," she said. "You playing dead. Playing zombie. Playing tennis, too. It *was* fun, wasn't it?"

"We can go camping again."

"I don't know if I'll ever be allowed out of the house." Mikey's smile stopped. "You know what?" she said. "I can't do it. I can't keep them from getting divorced."

"Sometimes you can't run things," Margalo said. "Sometimes there's just no difference anything you can do will make."

"Maybe," Mikey admitted. "Maybe. But I don't have to like it."

"And you don't," Margalo pointed out.

"Even if they can do it to me, I'm not going to let them make me like it."

"But things might be better once they're divorced. Better for you, I mean."

"Alone with her? You went to the mall with us. You know what it would be like. No, wait, she's got this boyfriend, so we won't be alone. Did you know she had a boyfriend?"

"I thought maybe."

"Why didn't I?" Mikey demanded.

A few cars went by, but none of them was Aurora's Nova wagon. None of them stopped to pick up Margalo.

"I never thought," Mikey announced glumly, "that I would look forward to going to school. But at least at school I can get away from this divorce stuff."

"You can run away to school, every day," Margalo said, looking on the bright side.

"Not every day. Not weekends," Mikey argued.

II.

Not So Bad an Ending

Margalo tossed her stuff into the rear of the Nova as she got into the backseat. Aurora and Steven were in a hurry, to pick up the little kids and see how everyone was and be home again. As they drove off, Margalo looked back at Mikey. Mikey was scuffing around on the sidewalk, in no hurry. Mikey already knew how everyone was.

Steven was driving. "Good weekend?" he asked, looking at her in the mirror.

"It was okay," Margalo said, noncommittal.

"How come you were right there, waiting?"

"She knew we'd be in a hurry," Aurora answered. "But what were you doing with a sleeping bag?"

"We slept out," Margalo said.

"It wasn't too cold for you?" Aurora asked. She turned to smile at Steven and tell Margalo, "Last night, by the end of the reception, I wished I'd worn a long-sleeved dress. Or brought a sweater. Steven was all right, he was wearing a suit — "

"I offered you my jacket."

"After we'd left the party you did. If I hadn't been cold, I could have danced hours longer. *I could have danced all night*," Aurora sang.

"*You could have danced all night*," Steven sang in agreement.

"Good wedding?" Margalo asked unnecessarily.

"Yes, even though I wish she'd let me bring my children. But it was fun anyway, wasn't it, Steven?"

"Admit it, Aurora, we had a good time having no children. It's nice to get away once in a while, good for both of us," Steven said.

"Actually," Margalo said, leaning forward so her face was between them. They were holding hands, across the gear box. "Actually, Mrs. Elsinger is mad at me. Well, really at Mikey, but she blames me, too. Mikey's grounded for a month. So — I can't go over there anyway, but she said I wasn't welcome in her house."

This surprised Aurora. "Whatever did you two get up to? I know Patty has a temper, but — and I'm not saying this to belittle your friendship, Margalo — but I'm pretty sure it's easier for Patty when Mikey has a friend over. That's the impression I get, because then Mikey's out of her hair. So I can't imagine why she'd try to keep you apart."

Margalo knew that. Aurora couldn't imagine, and didn't really have much interest in finding out. For one hopeful second, Margalo wondered if maybe her parents could never find out; because when they did, she'd be in bad trouble, probably the most she'd ever been in with them.

The only question was: Was it smart to tell them herself, tell them first, tell them right now?

But what if they never? The possibility tempted her. They might never. They weren't friends with the Elsingers, and who else would tell them? Who'd it hurt if they never found out?

"Mrs. Elsinger didn't know we were sleeping out," Margalo said. "Although," Margalo added, "she did know that we were safe. She didn't have to worry."

Which didn't make what Gianette had done any more forgivable. It just made things convenient for

Margalo. Gianette still deserved the worst thing Mikey could do to her, or Margalo could think up for Mikey to do.

"Are you upset about this?" Steven asked.

"Not really." Not yet, and not ever if being exiled from the Elsingers' house was all the punishment she got.

"Then everything's all right," Aurora said. "What do you say we pick up Esther first? Or Howie first, then Esther? And then when we get to your parents' for the little ones — "

"Don't forget Susannah and David, too," Steven said.

"I don't," she assured him. "You were the one who would have forgotten to get them presents. I'm the one who remembered. But we aren't opening any presents until we're home," she said.

"You brought presents?" Margalo asked.

"Nothing exciting," Aurora told her.

"Especially for you bigger children," Steven added.

"It won't be worth your while to have any hurt feelings," Aurora said.

"Okay, I won't," Margalo said. She sat back in the seat. "I'm lucky you two are my parents," she said, and knew it was true for more reasons than that she might stay out of trouble today.

"Compared to Anders and Patty? I don't blame you," Steven said.

He signaled, then turned left into an apartment complex.

"Anders is kind of sweet," Aurora protested. "I kind of like him. He might do better when he's out from under the marriage, don't you think? Do we know any women he might get along with? Don't laugh at me, Steven, I do know something about people."

They picked up Howie, then Esther, and the car was full. When David and Susanna and Stevie and Lily got gathered in too, the car would be too small. But they knew that, and they knew how they would handle it: Lily would sit on her mother's lap; Stevie would sit on David's lap; and Esther and Margalo — because they were the youngest unlappable children — would hunch in among the luggage at the rear of the station wagon and complain.

Margalo and Mikey didn't have a chance to talk again until the next day at school. "The first thing I'm going to do is beat her up," Mikey announced as Margalo got off the bus, "and make her give me back my money."

"Aren't you afraid of the *belle-dame*'s magic spells?" Margalo teased. Mikey didn't bother to respond.

The sky was cloudy and the air chilled. Being October, it might rain and it might not, but in case it did, most of the students from the older grades lingered outside until the very last minute.

"Do you know what bus she rides?" Mikey asked. "Hey, Tanisha, what bus is Gianette on?"

"Dunno," Tanisha answered. "Ask Linny. She's around back, I think."

But Mikey couldn't be bothered to search out Linny. She had more to tell Margalo. "They're doing it. Separating. A legal separation. She's moving in with her boyfriend. Today. She says it's all my fault, because of this weekend. All our fault, yours, too. Because I caused a crisis. He says I just brought things to a head."

Margalo wasn't about to ask the next question. She didn't want to have to hear the answer.

"They must like fighting," Mikey said. She showed her teeth, smiling. "They were still at it when I went to bed. Of course, I did go to bed at six thirty."

"I don't blame you."

"I was going to call you, but I'm grounded on the phone, too."

"Could you go to sleep that early?" Margalo asked.

Another big yellow bus pulled in. Children of all ages — all ages from five to thirteen, that is — rushed down the metal steps and up the broad cement sidewalk. Gianette wasn't one of them.

"At six thirty? Not on your life. But don't you want to know?"

Margalo played dumb. "Know what?"

"What they said."

"I know what they said," Margalo told Mikey. "I've already heard what they had to say."

"No, about me. About what will happen to me. Because they asked me what I wanted, because Dr. Taylor told them they should consider what I want." Mikey hesitated, smiled again with a flashing of teeth, and commented, "I don't think I *want* to know why he had to tell them that."

"What did you tell them?"

"What do you think?"

"Cut it out, Mikey. Just tell me."

"I told them all I want is to not change schools. I told them, I don't care which one of them I live with. So my father said he'd be willing to stay on in Newtown. She's transferring to the bank's city office, but it's okay because it's a lateral move, so she's not angry about that. I don't know if her boyfriend's going with her, or not. She said she'll miss me, and I can come for weekends, and you can, too. So that's okay. Anyway, I'm not going anywhere."

Mikey stared at Margalo, waiting for her reaction. Margalo wanted to stay cool about it, but when Mikey's words went into her head, not just in her ears — so glad, and relieved, she wanted to run a lap around the playground like a runner who has just taken first place in the race running her victory lap — even though Margalo hated running, especially in races — she shifted her feet. Mikey moved back. "Don't hug me," she said.

"Why would I hug you?" Margalo demanded crossly, because that, too, had crossed her mind.

"I'm not going to live in the same house, though. They can't afford to keep it without two salaries. But he's not staying at his same awful job, either, so he'll be looking for work. My mother," Mikey announced gleefully, "is going to have to pay him child support."

The bell rang then, to call them to homeroom. They hadn't laid eyes on Gianette.

Gianette wasn't in school that Monday, or the Tuesday, either. On Wednesday word went around the sixth-grade classes that Gianette St. Etienne had been withdrawn from school. Doucelle heard from her mother that Gianette had moved back to Louisiana. Mrs. Scott taught art at George Washington Elementary, so Doucelle always had the inside scoop on things. Gianette's grandmother had told Miss Carter, the school secretary, about Gianette moving back to Louisiana, when Miss Carter telephoned to be sure that Gianette wasn't playing hookey. On Thursday, Doucelle reported that the police had come to Miss Carter's office. "During music, while we were all in music yesterday. There were two of them in a squad car. Gianette was a shoplifter," Doucelle reported. "The store camera caught her doing it. She was taking lipsticks."

"Lipsticks?" Mikey asked. "What a waste. You'd think she'd take CDs, or at least something to eat, or rings, something she could sell. I would. How hard is it to shoplift shoes?" she asked, thinking about how if she had to live on her father's income, she might not have money for good sneakers.

"Doesn't it make you wonder about who was doing the stealing around here?" Margalo asked the group.

"But he stole from Gianette, too," Linny pointed out.

"He? Why not she?" Mikey demanded. "Who says a girl couldn't do it?"

"I was thinking about that, and if I were stealing from people, I'd steal from myself, too. For a cover," Margalo suggested.

Annaliese and LJ were convinced by Margalo's theory, and Linny couldn't argue it down, although she thought stealing was the kind of thing a certain Louis Caselli would do. "Smart thinking" was Ronnie's opinion of what Margalo had said.

"You can't steal from yourself," Mikey pointed out.

"You know what I mean," Margalo said.

Mikey did, and Margalo knew it.

Mikey had her own more interesting news, which had nothing to do with Gianette. "He called the ASPCA," she announced to Margalo. "They said they'd look into it. So maybe that fox will get freed after all."

"Maybe that fox's whole life has already been ruined," Margalo announced right back. "Even if it gets freed. Because it was kept in captivity."

"Maybe," Mikey said. "I know. But maybe not, too. Nobody knows everything," she pointed out to Margalo.

"Dunhh," Margalo agreed.

"Nobody's really in control of things," Mikey

pointed out, as if Margalo hadn't told her that a thousand times. "Not even me. Although I should be. I'm good at it." She waited for Margalo to open her mouth and start to say something really sarcastic, before she added, "That's a joke."

It took another week and more for the best part of Gianette's story to get told. Derrie saw an article in the newspaper that talked about a child-placement ring. It was a statewide welfare scam. The article said there were children who were sent to live with people who wanted to increase the amount of their welfare checks. The people would pay money, and they would be sent children they could register as dependents. The children stayed only long enough to get put onto the welfare rolls; then they moved out, like Gianette did with her *belle-dame* probably fake grandmother. After they'd gotten on the rolls, the children were moved to new homes, in different states.

"What a horrible way to live," Ronnie said. "You'd always be changing schools."

Annaliese agreed. "How can her parents let her do this? What about her father?"

"Probably the parents are the ones behind this," Derrie suggested.

"Rent-A-Kid," Tanisha said.

"I think it's sad. Imagine if you had to be one of those children? You'd feel like somebody's animal, somebody's property. It's practically slavery."

"There are worse things," Ann Tarwell told them.

They all knew that. They watched the news, they read the papers, they weren't uninformed about the really horrible things that could happen to kids. "That doesn't make it any better," they argued. "Just because it could be worse." Ann agreed with that. They realized, "You'd never have a chance to have any friends."

"Probably," Ronnie speculated, "she'll end up in jail. She doesn't have much of a chance if she's already probably stealing and definitely shoplifting. I don't know if I really liked her, but I feel sorry for her. If she came back — "

"I'd deck her," Mikey said, with feeling.

Everybody laughed.

Mikey laughed too, but she insisted, "I would."

As she and Margalo walked away, Margalo asked, "How much money did Gianette make, just from us? There was ten from you."

"Forty from my parents, and that nickel, too. Fifty-oh-five," Mikey said.

"She was practically a professional criminal,

wasn't she? And you know what, Mikey? We got her."

"Only once."

"And she couldn't con us like she did the rest. She couldn't beat us either."

"Nope," Mikey agreed, pleased with herself and Margalo. "Although she did make fifty dollars off of us. She was really good at being really bad."

"Yeah," Margalo agreed. "We have a lot to learn from her."

"You're joking, aren't you? Is that a joke?"

"I can't tell," Margalo said.

And finally Mikey got around to asking Margalo, "What did you get for punishment?" Hers had been kept the same, even though her mother had moved out; except that after the month's grounding, Margalo would be able to come over again, just like before. "What did they say?" Mikey asked.

"Nothing."

"Nothing? Nothing at all? Even for Aurora, that's pretty lenient. What did you tell her?"

"Nothing."

Mikey was stopped dead in her tracks. "They don't know?"

Margalo shook her head.

"But that's so risky."

Margalo nodded her head.

"What if they find out?"

"I only did it to help you out. It isn't like I really ran away."

"You're so — " Mikey said, filled with admiration, and jealous, too. "I mean, that's like — like a midcourt shot for a basket. I mean — what a move, Margalo. I hope you get away with it."

"Me too," Margalo said. After all, it wouldn't be fair for her to get punished for being a good friend, would it?